# Hummingbird

# Kisses

# Delia Latham

# Table of Contents

Dear Reader…

Heritage can be a wonderful thing—or not a good thing at all.

Not everyone is into genealogy. Others dig deep to find their ancestors and learn about their bloodline. But, history buff or not, a family's bloodline has a way of showing up. Body shape, facial features, hair and eye color…even personality quirks get passed on from generation to generation. I see expressions and mannerisms in my children that are incredibly like those of family members who are no longer with us—some of whom my children never met. This tells me that our ways of thinking and methods of expressing ourselves are not only learned but "built in"—little remnants of ancestry that make us who we are.

In Hummingbird Kisses, Toni's appearance indicates her Native American bloodline. She's a thoroughly modern woman who lives entirely in the present. She doesn't cling to the ways and beliefs of her ancestral tribe, but neither does she discount them as foolish or ignorant. She treasures the things she learned from her mother, but leans most heavily on the teachings of her Father—the One she calls Daddy God.

She's chosen wisely.

If who we are in this life shows a kinship to the God who breathed life into our beings…the One who loves each of us with an extraordinary, unfathomable love…our Creator…the giver of joy, the bringer of peace…the one and only God and Father of all, Jesus Christ—if others see Him in us, then our lives serve a purpose, and we can be proud of our godly heritage. It is an incredible honor to be part of the family of God.

I am deeply touched that you're spending a little of your precious time with me, Dear Reader. May you find something within these pages to encourage your heart, refresh your soul, and make you glad you chose to step into Toni Littlebird's world.

*Delia Latham*

# Reader Comments

"…such a moving story that I find myself, an hour or so after finishing the book, still feeling that deep emotional connection with the story."

~Phyllis Helton (**amongthereads.net**) on *A Christmas Beau*

"…a sweet and refreshing story of love and faith with a little bit of mystical charm."

~Gloria Anderson on *Winter Wonders*

"I can see this book as a Hallmark Movie."

~Ann on *Winter Wonders*

"…it was almost like watching a movie. I could see the things that were happening."

~Andrea Stephens on *Autumn Falls*

"I found myself amazed to discover that while reading, I was also praying! I've never known reading a book could be so uplifting."

~Paula Rose Michelson on *Autumn Falls*

"The visual imagery is superb and it draws you into the tender moments, the uplifting moments, and the inspiring moments equally and, in some instances, with life altering impact."

~Reviewed by Deborah Stone for Readers' Favorite

on *Summer Dreams*

"I would have given this book a 6 out 5 stars if I could."

~Deb Chatley on *Spring Raine*

"I love Delia Latham's writing; she brings scenes to life with flawless prose and beautiful descriptions."

~Kathleen Friesen on *The First Noelle*

"I had such fun reading this story, I was sad it had to end."

~Stacy Monson on *Bells on Her Toes*
(Love at Christmas Inn, Book 4)

"the power of love, and the power of prayer coupled with God's power are perfectly blended in a story and romance that left me cheering, and eagerly awaiting Delia's next release!"

~Marianne T. Evans on *Love in the WINGS*

"You can feel God's love wrap around you as you read this story."

~Donna Basinow on *Lexi's Heart*

"Delia Latham has a gift for creating engaging, magnetic characters and a charming setting where heavenly encounters unfold."

~Nancee Marchinowski on *Jewels for the Kingdom*

"It's full of taunting twists and turns laced with the supernatural and has mysteries within mysteries that my mind kept chewing on, clicking pieces of the puzzle together as I moved from chapter to the next."

~Angelia Phillips on *Goldeneyes*

# HUMMINGBIRD KISSES

## Copyright 2018
## Delia Latham

Published by Heavens Touch Books

ISBN: 978-1983913679
First Edition, 2018
Published in the United States of America

Contact information:

Delia Latham: delia@delialatham.net

# Dedication

To Lottie-dah, who shares my love for
hummingbirds, and is a special bright spot in my life,
just like these beautiful, fascinating little gifts from God.

# About the Book

Toni Littlebird believes God has created someone especially for her. When it's time, He will bring him to her. When she meets him, she'll know that he's The One, and she will love him in that very moment.

But that's before Dax Hendrick roars into Hummingbird Hollow on a noisy, crippled Harley, spitting stinky filth into the air and chasing away Toni's beloved hummingbirds. Dax sports a wild mop of dark hair, an unkempt beard, and a maddening propensity to turn everything into a smile—even when Toni doesn't want to smile. She takes one look into his mesmerizing blue-green eyes and...she knows. This uncivilized creature with too much hair and an offensively loud mode of transportation is "The One." She'd been right about knowing him in an instant, but wrong about something far more important: She will never love him.

Why God sent Dax to this beautiful place is a mystery, and it's clear he can't expect any answers from the lovely but unsympathetic owner of Inn the Hollow—a haphazardly constructed dwelling that goes against every professional rule in Dax's area of expertise. He hopes to get the green light on getting out of there before the uneven corners, crooked floor slats, and random construction wither his architectural creativity.

Is it possible that, between God's gentle leading and a lesson or two from the fascinating hummingbirds that populate the hollow, Dax and Toni will open their hearts to each other? Or will their stubborn wills ruin God's beautiful gift of love?

<sup>7</sup>But ask the animals, and they will teach you,
or the birds in the sky, and they will tell you;
<sup>9</sup>Which of all these does not know
that the hand of the Lord has done this?
Job 12:7,9

# 1

"GOOD MORNING, LITTLE ONE." TONI Littlebird spoke softly to the tiny creature perched on her outstretched hand. As always, a thrill of pleasure coursed through her blood at the simple but exhilarating contact. "Aren't you a beauty!"

The hummingbird cocked his head one way and then the other. When another hummer landed on Toni's opposite shoulder, his wings fluttered with the lightning speed typical of his species but then settled again without further protest.

Toni laughed—a gentle purr of delight that wouldn't frighten her little feathered friends.

"That's right…be nice. I know you guys like to guard your turf, but here in the hollow, you're on my territory. You're all welcome, and I'll not have you running each other off."

As if they understood every word, the hummers seemed content to allow each other a bit of space. Within moments, small jewel-toned birds lined both of Toni's arms and shoulders. A couple of them nestled into the palms of her hands.

She continued a stream of quiet conversation…a variation of the same words she spoke to her tiny visitors every day. A few she addressed by names she'd given them, though she could never explain how she recognized those few hummingbirds apart from the others.

"I must go inside, my sweet darlings. The Coming Up Valentines Dinner and Dance is tonight, so there's a lot to be done today. Will you all be on your best behavior for my guests, please? Diamond, you keep the peace out here, OK?

Sapphire will help, won't you, sweetness?"

She gently lifted her arms and, as a matter of routine, began to turn in gentle, swaying circles, honoring her hummingbirds in what she thought of as a ritual "see you later" dance. Eyes closed, she drank in the warmth of the sun on her face and the near-zero weight of the birds lining her arms and riding her shoulders. Her favorite part of every morning was this time spent with the lovely, fascinating birds who so inexplicably loved the hollow and her gardens as much as she did.

But this time her dance wasn't destined for the customary slow-to-a-standstill finale—the gentle farewell to the birds, who always remained in place as she danced, never lifting off to soar away until she'd blown kisses and spoken soft, loving words of goodbye.

Instead, an ugly roar split the air. Distant at first, it became more abrasive and disruptive with every moment. Loud music accompanied the discordant, mechanical growl. As the noisy intrusion reached a decibel of such intensity that Toni's ears ached, the tiny birds on her arms and shoulders first began to tremble—despite her quiet reassurances—then lifted and darted away, almost as one.

A sudden, overwhelming chemical smell filled the air. Toni's hands flew to her face, but covering her nose didn't reduce the unpleasant odor. The distinct stench of oil and gas billowed over and around the house in a noxious cloud. Never had Hummingbird Hollow been subject to such odorous and ear-crunching company!

Toni rushed toward the inn, her jaw set, spine rigid and unyielding. Whomever had wrecked her meditation time with the hummingbirds deserved a proper tongue-lashing, and she wouldn't hesitate to give them exactly that. How dare anyone intrude on her treasured morning interlude with her tiny, winged friends?

She blew through the kitchen, ignoring the wide-eyed, questioning glances of the kitchen staff. On she went, past a formal dining room and the huge common room with its impressive rock fireplace. Today she didn't give the striking floor-to-ceiling feature a fleeting glance.

An over-sized entrance served as the sign-in space for her bed and breakfast, Inn the Hollow. She flew through the archway and zoomed across the floor toward the door, which opened just as she reached it. Toni catapulted into a big, broad, unyielding chest covered in black leather.

"Oh!" She bounced backward, but was saved the indignity of falling on her backside when a strong arm circled her waist and pulled her against the leather-covered chest once again.

"Whoa! Can't have you falling for me like that." Amusement lent pleasant undertones to a deep voice that rumbled like silent thunder in the chest against which Toni's body was pinned. For an inexplicable moment, she found herself longing to simply stay there, held in those strong arms, with the smell of male sweat and warm leather filling her senses.

She gasped and pushed herself away. The contact suddenly felt disturbingly intimate.

"Don't flatter yourself. You were in my way, and besides, I'm pretty sure you're the one who interrupted my morning meditation and frightened my friends away."

Despite her own respectable five-foot, eight-inch frame, Toni found she needed to look up to make eye contact. Right now, she could see nothing but that broad, leather-covered chest. The fact that she was reluctant to look elsewhere stoked the fire of anger already lit within her. She jerked her traitorous gaze upward, and found, instead of a neck, a long, rather unkempt, dark blonde beard.

Ugh. Facial hair. She'd never found it attractive—probably something to do with her Native American ancestry—so she continued her visual journey, but slammed on mental brakes in the next instant. Between the beard and mustache that surrounded them, an amused half smile claimed full, well-defined lips, the lower of which was fuller and even more sensual than the upper. Fascinated, Toni found herself reluctant to look away—until those perfect lips twitched further upward in obvious amusement.

Allowing her gaze to move on past an impossibly straight nose, Toni bit back a gasp when she met a pair of startling blue-green eyes. Kind, gentle, fun-loving eyes that reached out and touched her soul. They were *the* eyes. The ones she'd known, without being able to describe, would someday turn her world upside down. Eyes that belonged to *him*—the man God had created just for her. The man she'd always said she'd know when she looked into his eyes.

This man...whoever he was.

Her heart sank. This man...who'd interrupted the peaceful tranquility she so loved about Hummingbird Hollow. This man...who boasted long, untended, dark golden-brown strands—on his chin, on his head, and hanging several inches down his back.

This man, whose name she didn't yet know, and whose entrance into her life had been anything but romantic, was God's choice of a life partner for LiTonya Littlebird, better known as Toni, who owned and operated Hummingbird Hollow's bed and breakfast, Inn the Hollow.

Toni sighed. *God never makes a mistake. His choice is always right.* Things she'd been taught all her life and believed with all her heart. Still, in this telling moment, she couldn't help but wonder. Surely, Lord, you didn't intend to send me this...this barbarian!

4

Having smoothed her top and brushed off her slacks with slow movements and trembling fingers, she lifted her gaze, determined to appear strong and, most importantly, unshaken by the powerful revelation. With her anger tamped a mere hair by shock, Toni crossed her arms and took a backward step away from the mountainous man in her doorway.

"Well, whatever horse you rode in on needs to be given a proper burial. It's stinking up my hollow. Tell me what I can do for you, so you can get that thing out of here. I can only hope the stench clears before my guests arrive tonight."

Right out of an Indian fairy tale!

Despite the twin circles of outrage on the woman's cheeks, Dax Hendrick found it quite impossible to remove his gaze from her face. She epitomized beauty. Pure, undefiled, completely natural beauty. This creature, whom he'd held in the circle of his own arms, was the stuff of every man's most creative imagination.

Perfection. He'd found perfection, embodied in this raven-haired woman who could only be of Native American descent. The high cheekbones and blue-black hair bespoke her heritage.

But what of those eyes? Not black, but not brown either. Not green. Somewhere between the three colors, and nearly translucent, her gaze held the power to hypnotize and mesmerize. Dax fought the urge to stare into them as if searching for the meaning of life.

"Well?" She snapped her fingers a few inches from his nose. "Are you going to tell me your name, and why you've disturbed the peace of Hummingbird Hollow? I'll have to pray a million prayers to cleanse the stink from my home."

"A million? That's a bit of an exaggeration, don't you think? Do your gods truly require such an over-abundance of pleading before they answer? Because, if so, I can introduce you to—"

"I serve Jesus Christ, stranger, and you are correct—I misspoke. He answers my every sincere prayer, and there is no need to repeat my sincere petitions again." Those lovely, indescribable eyes glittered across the counter behind which she'd hidden her graceful form. "I guess I'm a little shaken by your thunderous entrance. Between the blaring cacophony you probably call music, and the roar of your engine, I fear my beloved hummingbirds will never make another appearance in this hollow."

Dax opened his mouth, but she didn't give him a chance to speak.

"If you'll tell me how I can help you get back on the road, I'll be happy—more than happy—to get you on your way."

He couldn't take his eyes off the beautiful proprietress, whose blood clearly ran about as warm as a rattlesnake's. How was it even possible for such astounding beauty to exist in the same vessel with a vitriolic personality of this degree?

Maybe he'd made a mistake, and this big, haphazardly designed residence wasn't the one he'd seen with disturbing regularity in recent meditative moments. Maybe another, similar hollow existed somewhere in Arkansas, and he'd simply made a mistake. Surely this one, though downright beautiful, couldn't be the same peaceful little vale he'd seen in every prayer picture he'd been shown for the past six months.

Except it was, and he knew it.

"Well?" The woman drummed her fingernails—clean and well-shaped, but not fake in any way—on the countertop. "I really don't have all day, sir." When she spoke again, uncertainty softened the edges of her previously acerbic tone. "Can I help you in some way?"

Dax stood for a moment longer, studying the woman...and his surroundings, which were tastefully decorated and receptive, despite the absence of professional planning and design. Walls jutted off from one another in a sad lack of symmetry. Corners didn't always meet in perfect harmony, which grated Dax's nerves and left him vaguely nauseated. Whoever had built this structure hadn't known a thing about architecture. And yet someone—probably the breathtaking lady who stood frowning at him across the counter—had managed to make it warm, welcoming, and pleasing to the casual eye.

Now if only he possessed such a thing. The only way he knew to look at any structure with walls was purely professional, always assessing the good points and bad ones.

He pulled in a deep breath and held it a few seconds. When he felt certain he could respond with any kind of grace, he smiled. The woman was like a stunning desert cactus—lovely to the eye, but painful to the touch.

"Yes, ma'am. I'd like to claim my reservation, if you don't mind."

A soft gasp and a slight widening of the eyes gave away her surprise. "You...have a reservation? Here? At Inn the Hollow?"

At his nod, she ran a finger down one of the pages in an open registry on the counter. At last, she raised her gaze—which bordered on repentant—to his.

"Are you Dax Hendrick?"

"I am."

"And I—" She broke off and nibbled at her lip. A small storm brewed in her eyes. "I apologize."

Dax grinned, impressed with the woman's strong will and easy grace. "Then all is forgiven?"

Her level gaze held a world of...something. Something Dax found himself eager to explore.

"I wouldn't go that far, Mr. Hendrick. My hollow still smells like oil and gas, and my sweet hummingbirds are still hiding out somewhere in the trees. I can only pray they might return tomorrow." She laid a pen on the counter. "I'm Toni Littlebird. Welcome to my home. If you'll just sign the registry, sir. Will you be paying with cash or credit card?"

And just like that, she set the basis for their relationship. Professional. Honest to a fault. Well, he could handle that.

Except...those eyes of hers made him want to scratch "professional" off the list, and dive head first into "personal."

Oh, well. One couldn't have it all. Right now, he had a sick Harley to care for, and according to this woman, his ailing baby stank. So he had a little clean-up to do.

Dax carried his one duffel bag inside and checked out his room—clean, neat, and decorated with an eye to the owner's heritage. A large dreamcatcher hung over the bed. On the opposite wall, a colorful blanket, woven in a design that screamed Native American. A similar one draped the foot of the bed, and a luxurious fur rug added warmth and interest to the floor. He nodded once. This would do.

Yet his trained eye caught the slight imperfections—walls that weren't quite even, a telltale give in the floor due to discrepancies in measurement, or perhaps craftsmanship. Without meaning to do so, he noticed space-saving measures that had been overlooked. Then again, at the time this place was built, not a lot of consideration had been given to such things.

At the thought, a chuckle rumbled from between his lips. Who knew when it had been built? Without even searching out the structure's history, he knew that it was an architectural mutt—it had grown a wing here and a room there, over a good many years and quite a few owners, with little thought to aesthetics or proper building techniques. Various sections of the home spread every which direction from the central core. The result provided more living space—clearly the original intent—but brought no dynamics into play. Heating and cooling had to be major costs, given all the randomly added space. He doubted the place had central air and heat. Insulation? Certainly not a given. With all the faulty construction quirks, how could his hostess even afford to keep the doors open?

Not his problem. He tossed his duffel into a small closet, took a moment to splash water in his face and wash his hands, then headed back downstairs. He'd take a quick walk to stretch his legs, and maybe find some out-of-the-way place where he could hide his ugly, stinky Harley until he got it back in shape.

# 2

**TONI WAVED AND SMILED AT** yet another guest across the patio, and then slipped through the back door into the kitchen. How had the crowd gotten so large...and why were her guests being served so slowly?

Two women worked alongside Chef Jonathan Savage—a handsome Native American with a gentle heart as big as the man himself. No mean feat, considering Jon stood a full six feet and several inches, with broad shoulders and an imposing frame. His skills in the kitchen were unsurpassed, and Toni gave him full credit for many of the five-star reviews her guests posted online for the B & B. She couldn't imagine trying to run the place without the big guy.

At night, Jon's presence in the guest quarters off the kitchen gave her a sense of safety and security. Not that she was any kind of shrinking violet. The boldness and bravery of her ancestors still flowed strong within her blood, but neither was she a fool. Many people reserved their rooms weeks or months ahead, via phone or email. While Toni possessed a highly tuned, almost supernatural ability to judge character, that skill served her best when looking a person straight in the eye. Modern technology, while beneficial in many ways, left her unable to turn down a customer because she sensed something in them that made her wary or uncomfortable. Jon's presence on site made her far more at ease with that necessity.

An almost palpable buzz filled the kitchen tonight, and Jon was in full chef mode. He stood with his back to the door, slicing a large ham into impossibly thin segments. His two chef's assistants barely took time to breathe between tasks. Mara, a petite woman with skin the color of dark caramel, looked too delicate to be of much help, but she didn't so much as groan as she hefted a large pan of scalloped potatoes onto a long stainless-steel table. Almost in the same movement, she slid a serving spoon from a drawer underneath. In a blink, neat helpings of potatoes appeared in a row of plates lined up beside the oversized pan.

Across from the delicately built Mara, a generously endowed, large-boned woman filled salad plates with the patented Honeysuckle Hollow spinach salad garnished with ham, mango and strips of prosciutto, and drizzled with an incredible pomegranate vinaigrette. Of few words and many intimidating expressions, Carla Godney's iron gray hair lived in a perpetual bun atop her head. She had worked in this kitchen long before the house became a business. As a little girl, and the only child on the premises, Toni had spent much of her time with this woman. Despite her rather off-putting appearance and persona, Carla loved children, and considered them the only true innocents in a rapidly devolving world. She it was who'd accompanied little Toni on lengthy explorations of the hollow, introduced her to the local flora and fauna, and taught her to be mannerly and kind.

Toni's mother, Gentle Willow, had possessed a loving spirit...and a fragile, delicate body. Unable physically to handle much exertion, she'd been forced—to her own intense sorrow—to trust others with the care of her daughter. Carla's willingness to take Toni under her wing had been a blessing to both mother and child.

As for her father...well, Toni hadn't a clue. She'd never known him, and her mother never spoke of him. In answer to Toni's questions, she always gave the same response. "Some men are not meant to be daddies, LiTonya. Do not shed tears for his absence. Instead, be thankful for God's constant presence. He is the only Father you'll ever need."

Perhaps because it was delivered so matter-of-factly, without a hint of malice or resentment, Toni soon came to take her mother's answer to heart. Now, as the adult owner of the only home within the hollow, Toni never wasted a moment mourning the absence of a father figure in her life. God was her Father, and she felt His love so palpably...had come to know Him on an intimate basis. She often referred to Him as Daddy God. So far, He hadn't tossed a lightning bolt her way, or consumed the hollow in heavenly fire, so she assumed He didn't mind. Who knew? Perhaps He even cherished the title, recognizing it as the term of adoration Toni intended it to be.

But she had no time to stand here reflecting on her life. She had a crowd of people waiting for food that wasn't arriving at their tables fast enough.

Although Jon faced away from her, he seemed to sense her presence in the room. He tossed a quick smile over one shoulder. "Sorry things are moving a little sluggishly, boss. Peter and Meli were involved in a bit of a smash-up on the way here tonight. They're both OK, but they're being held a few hours for observation. Mara and Carla are going back and forth between washing dishes and putting the plates together."

Toni swallowed a sigh and reached for an apron. "What can I do to help?"

Without turning her way, Jon chuckled. "To start with, you can leave that apron where it is."

Toni caught Mara's intake of breath. The chef's ability to sense what was going on in the room around him occasionally shivered the other workers. Carla didn't blink an eye, and Toni simply thanked God for the man's sensitivity to his surroundings. It made him an excellent overseer in the kitchen, a super-focused bodyguard, and a reliable and trusted friend.

"I have to help. We've got to get these people served."

Long brown fingers appeared over Toni's right shoulder and snagged the apron from between her fingers. "I've got this, Miss Littlebird. You get out there and play hostess."

The deep, rumbling voice sent Toni's heart on an all-out race, and clenched her tummy tight as a knot. She whirled around and caught her breath. Her most recent guest had trimmed his unruly beard to a quite presentable size and shape. His long hair, tamed into smooth, gleaming strands, was fastened at the nape of his neck. He'd even dressed for dinner. In dark slacks and a bright blue dress shirt with the top buttons open, no indication remained of the unkempt man who had roared into the hollow just this morning.

As Toni watched, still trying to take in the man's transformation, he wrapped the apron strings around his waist and tied them in a passable bow behind his back.

"You—you can't be in here, Mr. Kendrick."

"Dax, and why not?" He nodded at Jon across the room, and Toni made a mental note to chew on the chef later about that twinkle in his eyes. "I've already eaten, and I'm at loose ends. Point me in the right direction. I wouldn't be much of a server, but dirty dishes—hey, that I can do."

To Toni's horror, Jon hooked a thumb toward the double sinks in the back corner. "We can sure use the help, dude. That corner's all yours."

Dax winked at Toni, sauntered across the room and plunged his hands into the soapy water. "Hope y'all don't mind me singing while I work. I'm not Nashville material, but I don't see anybody covering their ears when I sing along with the crowd at church."

"Nobody minds a song around here." Jon placed the tray

of ham onto the table next to Carla and reached for a divided dish that held halved cherries and the pineapple slices he'd removed from the baked ham earlier. "If we're lucky, Toni might even join in. She's got a voice right out of the halls of Heaven."

Toni gasped as warmth rushed upward from her neck into her face. To Dax's credit, however, he didn't play on Jon's revelation to further her embarrassment.

"Nice to know. Maybe we can make that happen when things slow down a bit." All the while he washed dinner plates with surprising speed and dexterity. Why had she expected him to be clumsy and slow? Now he grabbed a dish towel and set to work drying the ones he'd washed. "Right now, judging by the number of plates in this sink, I'd say y'all need some clean ones PDQ." He lifted the stack of a dozen or so plates shoulder high, balanced them neatly on the tips of his fingers, and walked them over to Mara and Carla. "Here ya go, ladies. Fill 'em up." With a graceful pirouette, he returned to the corner and started on the next batch of dirty dinnerware.

Just like that, Dax Hendrick saved the day.

Toni shook her head. "Well, looks like I'm not needed in here after all." She cast one more glance toward the man standing over a sink full of dirty dishes. Who was this surprising, unpredictable person...besides God's choice for her? Where had he come from? Why was he here?

No answers dropped out of the blue, so she reluctantly made her way back to the crowded patio to mingle with her guests. Some outrageously curious and questioning part of her longed to return to the kitchen in case Dax really did burst into song. She'd love to hear what kind of voice came from within a creature so large...and toned...and achingly handsome.

Stop it. Right here, right now. Toni sternly reminded herself of Dax's status as a guest at Inn the Hollow. He'll be around a minute, and then he'll be gone. No need to start thinking he's something special. He was in no way special, not to her. Just a massive man with a big motorcycle, and lots of noise and stink followed him around. He'd drifted in. He'd drift back out in a day or two.

Thank God.

Dax dried the last dish, wiped down the sink and counter, and tossed his apron into a nearby basket of soiled linens.

"Thanks a whole boatload, man." The big chef, Jonathan, smiled from across the room. "I don't know how we'd have gotten through this thing without you. You're a lifesaver."

"Glad I could help." Dax grinned. He'd found a great deal of satisfaction in making sure the chef and his assistants had clean plates, bowls and glasses waiting when they needed them. In addition, he'd discovered a surprising rapport with Jonathan, and the two of them had kept up a steady stream of banter throughout the evening. Even after the teens arrived from their hospital visit—cheerfully showing off their minor cuts and bruises to a conciliatory Carla—he'd stayed to help out wherever Jon and the two women allowed his assistance. It'd been awhile since his days of kitchen work in college, and he'd enjoyed the brief re-visitation.

"How long you here for?" Jonathan joined Dax at the door.

"I'm not really sure. I booked the room for a week, but I probably won't need to stick around that long. We'll see."

"Well, I hope you get to stay a little longer. Maybe I could show you around a bit. Have you been into Eureka Springs?"

"As a matter of fact, it was a guy in Eureka Springs who

pointed me in the right direction to find this place. Interesting town. I'd love to see more of it."

"Then we'll do that. It's a special place. But then, so is the hollow. Lots of history in both locations."

"Sounds like a plan." He grinned. "We know where to find each other."

Jon pointed toward a door at the far end of the room. "That's my quarters. Come knocking whenever you're ready, or if I can help you with something."

"Actually…" Dax hiked an eyebrow. "There wouldn't be a place around here where I can hide my bike while I fix what's got her out of sorts, would there? She's just running a little rich—shouldn't take long to get 'er fixed up, but I don't want to create an eyesore out front while I'm at it."

Jonathan chuckled. "Yeah, probably not a great way to get on Toni's good side. She's the most amazing person I know, but she can be downright ferocious where this place is concerned. And the hummingbirds, of course." He shook his head and performed an elaborate eyeroll. "The man, woman or child who mistreats, threatens, or otherwise upsets those little critters is in danger of bringing out Toni Littlebird's inner tiger. She loves those hummers like they're her own babies."

Dax had gathered as much by his chilly reception earlier that day. "Well, I guess most folks find them fascinating."

"Sure, but it's more than that with Toni. She says they remind her that God is real, because…well, only He could create something so perfect, and so beautiful." Jonathan rubbed a hand over his smooth chin. "She has some kind of…strange…but really awesome connection with them, Dax. You'll laugh, but I swear it's true. Those little guys—they speak to her. Like they have their own language, you know? The birds and Toni."

Dax shot a quick, questioning glance at Jonathan, but the other man's expression showed not even the hint of a smile. Good for him.

"Well, I suppose if God can create a hummingbird, He is also well able to give that creature the ability to communicate with whomever He wills."

Jon slapped a hand on Dax's shoulder. "Good answer, my man. Good answer." He turned and headed off across the kitchen toward his quarters. Just as he reached the door, he swung around to enact a rather imperfect salute. "Thanks again for helping us get through the dinner without losing customers, to say nothing of stressing and humiliating Toni. And in answer to your question…yes. There's a storage shed out back that you can hide away in while you fix your ride. I'll take you there in the morning."

"That'll work. Good night."

Dax turned, thinking to go to his room, but just as quickly changed his mind and slipped through the door for a breath of air. As he stepped outside, faint strains of guitar music drifted across the still night. He followed it to a gazebo in the center of the garden, where Toni sat propped against the cushioned back of a bench, strumming the strings.

He opened his mouth to call out a greeting, but stopped when she began to sing. Something shivered along his spine. Her voice held a haunting, magical quality. Dax struggled to draw a breath. He eased back a step, and then another. If she knew he stood there, she'd stop singing…and he couldn't bear for that to happen.

She sang in a language he didn't know, but the distinct nuances of Native American speech patterns couldn't be missed. The melody was easily recognizable as Amazing Grace. Toni sang a verse and the chorus, then switched to English. By then, Dax had eased down onto the ground and lay back on the grass. He stared up at the sky—filled with a bazillion twinkling stars that looked close enough to reach out and grab a handful. With Toni singing that old, familiar tune under a sky like this one, created by the God to Whom she sang in a clear, pure voice that rang with sincerity, Dax's heart filled to bursting with gratitude and praise. How long had it been since he'd felt such a strong heavenly presence?

By the time the last note died out and Toni rose to go inside, Dax had given himself over to worship. He let her go inside without ever revealing his presence. For a long time, he lay there, staring up at the sky, breathing in the fresh air, and whispering soft praises into the night.

# 3

**"WHERE ARE THEY TAKING THAT** thing?"

From her balcony swing, Toni spotted Jonathan and Dax following a narrow footpath into the woods. Jonathan took the lead, and Dax followed…pushing a huge motorcycle. Toni shivered. She couldn't imagine riding on one of those noisy, two-wheeled monstrosities, especially at the speeds they traveled.

Still, to each his own. If her mother had taught her anything, it was to respect the personalities, likes and dislikes of other people—so long as they also remained respectful of God and others.

Despite herself, a smile teased at her lips at the thought of Dax with an apron around his waist and dishwater dripping from his elbows. What was it about washing dishes that brought even the biggest and toughest of men right down on a level with everyone else?

She needed to find a way to thank him for his help. Had he not stepped in to fill the gap left by Peter and Meli after their accident, last night's event would have ended on a far less positive note. He'd given freely of himself, and with good grace…despite the lack of welcome he'd received from her.

His disruptive arrival still rankled, and she had yet to find out if the hummingbirds would return. But she owed her guests better than what she'd given Dax. She couldn't yet bring herself to apologize. But she could do something to show her appreciation for his kindness in her moment of need.

She'd think of what that 'something' needed to be—just

not right this minute.

After a refreshing shower, she got dressed and headed to the gardens with a great deal of trepidation. What if her beautiful little friends had found greener, less noisy pastures?

Strolling through the rows of flowering shrubs and bushes, she kept a sharp eye out for the darting movements of small, winged creatures. Listened for the distinct hum created by the quick-fire beat of their wings. Prayed for their return.

After a few moments, she lowered herself onto the lawn and closed her eyes. Her mind went quiet, focused on the abundance of God's blessings around her. A gentle breeze brushed soft, trailing fingers against her cheek and through her hair. From the wooded area behind the inn, twitters and tweets filled the air. The honk of a larger bird sounded from somewhere above, momentarily hushing the song of the smaller species. A frog croaked from the pond behind the gardens.

The more Toni focused inward, the more she felt in tune with her outward surroundings. For a split second, she thought she heard the rustle of a blade of grass when it welcomed the lighting of a butterfly. The soil beneath the lawn shifted subtly as the sunshine warmed it for the new day.

At last she recognized a distinctive whirr of wings, and something flashed past her right ear in a rush of cool air. Still she didn't move. Soon she heard it again, a bit slower this time. The hummer's wings almost brushed her head. Once again, the buzz of approach, and then…the almost imperceptible touch on her shoulder when the bird landed.

She opened her eyes and moved one hand slowly upward, stopping just below the hummingbird's perch. A smile spread across her face when the little creature settled onto her palm.

"Good morning, my precious! I'm going to stand up now. Don't be frightened."

He remained in her hand with only a slight flutter of iridescent wings, and then Toni was on her feet. Within moments, hummers lined her arms and shoulders, nestled into both hands, even perched atop her head.

"I'm so sorry you were frightened yesterday, my little beauties. That was just Dax, and his ride was ill. He didn't mean to scare you away. I was worried you wouldn't come back at all."

One of the birds on her shoulder moved close to her ear. Tchip, tchip, tchip. Tchip, tchip. Tchuk.

"Aah! Well, thank you, Ruby-bright. I love all of you too…so very much. I should have known you'll always come back."

For a few more moments, she enjoyed the tranquil peace of the garden, and soft conversation with her beloved birds. But she didn't have time to dawdle.

"Well, my darlings. I have work to do, and I'm sure you do, as well. But I'll be back tomorrow…if it's still part of Daddy God's plan. I can't imagine starting a day without all of you to breathe peace into my spirit."

She began to sway, initiating the goodbye ritual with which she ended this part of every morning. The birds stayed with her as she whispered sweet words of love, interspersed with praises from the book of Psalms.

"I will praise You as long as I live, Daddy God. Thank You for the blessing of my beautiful little friends. Isn't He wonderful, my darlings? He turned my wailing to dancing, He clothed me with joy, so my heart could sing His praises. Just as each day brims with Your beauty, Lord—and yours, little ones!—my mouth brims with praise."

Eventually, she slowed to a stop, and eased her arms upward, and then down in a slow, graceful descent. Up once more, almost as if she was trying to fly.

"Off to your days now, my darlings. Daddy God be with you until I see you again."

Toni began to blow kisses toward the fascinating, tiniest of birds she loved so much. They rose upward and darted off, one at a time, then two or three. Finally, the last of the bunch—Diamond, Sapphire and Ruby-Bright—took their leave.

More than a few found their way to one bird bath or another. Others soared toward the many flowering bushes scattered around and throughout the garden area. Toni noted some activity at the nesters attached to half a dozen or so trees as well as a few posts the gardener had put in place at her request. The birds tugged cotton from behind the chicken wire that held it in place, then tucked it into small indentations in the wood. Before long, tiny eggs would nestle within those soft, cozy nests.

More beautiful hummers to grace Hummingbird Hollow.

"Have a blessed day, little ones," she whispered.

She turned to go inside, and then paused. Perhaps she'd take a stroll down the footpath and see what Jon and Dax were up to.

Then again…maybe not. Just thinking about her new guest tied her tummy into a tight, squirming ball. If God really intended her and Dax Hendrick to share a life, He needed to give her the ability to be around the man without turning her insides into a mass of jiggling gelatin. Anger had gotten her through their first encounter, and desperation through the second. Today she had neither going for her.

Probably best to just avoid the man altogether.

"Hey, Toni!"

Jon. So the men were back. She swung around, praying Dax had already gone to his room.

He hadn't. His teal gaze traveled her face, and something

in his expression set off a thousand danger signals.

"That was…incredible. I, uhm—" He cleared his throat, pulled in a breath and blew it out, slowly.

He saw me dance with the hummers.

Toni swallowed. Hard. Her cheeks warmed, but not from embarrassment. Not exactly. Her morning ritual was an intimate expression of her love for God, and for the hummingbirds. She'd never invited anyone to join her for what she called "meditation time."

"I'm…beyond impressed. That was the most beautiful thing I've ever seen. In my life. All of it. My whole life, I mean." Dax rolled his eyes, and a wave of brick red color crept from his neck upward—under his beard, and into his face.

Toni giggled. She couldn't help it.

Dax shot her a surprised glance. His eyebrows reached for each other over that perfect nose of his, and one deep crease formed across his forehead. "What—?"

Jonathan laughed outright. Toni tried not to join him, but one hand flew to her lips to cover the smile that would not be hidden. Despite her best intentions, a little burst of merriment made its way around her fingers.

Dax narrowed his gaze on her…and then he was laughing too.

"OK, you two. I get it. That wasn't nearly as smooth as I wanted it to be, but come on…it's the first time I've ever witnessed anything even remotely like that. Toni, I wish you could see for yourself how beautiful it was. You were dancing with those hummingbirds!"

"And…?" Toni grinned, enjoying the man's moment of discomfort, and not the least bit ashamed of her reaction.

"And, well, I think you were carrying on a conversation with them too." Dax hiked one eyebrow, looking a little uncertain. "W-were you?"

"Of course I was. It'd be a little rude not to speak with my dance partners, don't you think?"

"I guess—I mean, yeah, sure…uhm…"

"Okay, that's enough." Jonathan broke in, stopping Dax's painful attempt to communicate. "I think we've enjoyed ourselves enough at his expense. Dax is our guest, remember?" Jonathan gave the other man a light punch on the shoulder. "We came out here because he wanted to ask a favor of you. And since we made him our laughingstock, it wouldn't be very nice of you to deny his simple request, now would it?"

Toni tensed. "What kind of favor?"

Dax held up a hand. "Nothing outlandish—and you can say no…if you think you must."

Then he smiled. Toni bit down on her bottom lip. How was she supposed to say no to anything he asked, when he pulled out that kind of weapon? Even though her heart still shouted He's the one, everything else within her said Not this man. Her emotions seemed determined to take her up and down and sideways every time they came in contact.

Which could only mean one thing. Given her mental confusion and emotional turmoil where he was concerned, she needed to stay as far from him as possible, extending only the same courtesy all of her guests received. No more, no less.

"What is it you need, Mr. Hendrick? We strive to keep our guests happy and comfortable here in the Hollow. I'll do whatever I can for you…within reason."

"Just Dax, and thank you." He dipped his chin once before capturing her gaze with his own. "Jon says you mentioned going into Eureka Springs this morning. Any chance I can ride along? I need to buy a part for my loud, stinky horse."

Dax thought about calling the "turnabout is fair play" rule and laughing out loud at the look on Toni's face. But he'd been taught to be a gentleman and couldn't bring himself to take pleasure in her obvious discomfort. She would say no, of course. She still didn't like him too much, despite her effort to be polite to a guest.

He'd given it the old heave-ho anyway. Now all he could do was hope he hadn't put out too much heave and a hair too little ho.

"Toni?" Jon wasn't laughing anymore. Concern edged his voice when Toni just stood there, nibbling at her bottom lip. Even that looked good...downright adorable, actually...on Toni Littlebird. "You okay, boss?"

She blinked—twice, and then quite visibly donned a smile. Dax hiked one eyebrow. He wasn't sure he'd ever before literally watched a person do that...put on a smile, like an article of clothing that fit a hair too snug for comfort.

"Sorry, Jon, I got a little distracted." She tilted her head toward Dax. "I suppose I owe you, since you spent an entire evening slaving away in my kitchen."

Dax frowned. Could she be any less gracious?

"You don't owe me anything, Miss Littlebird." The words came out a bit clipped, and he made no effort to change his tone. Drop-dead gorgeous or not, the lady had crossed a line. "I helped in the kitchen because I saw a need. I didn't ask for or expect payment, and I won't accept any—even in the form of a ride into town."

Toni's eyes went wide, and she bit down on her lip again. This time, Dax failed to see the charm in the habitual gesture.

"I'll walk." He shook his head and returned her close-lipped smile that was not a smile. "Enjoy your drive."

He strode across the lawn toward the inn.

"Wow, boss." Jon spoke quietly, but still, Dax heard.

Confusion and disappointment edged his new friend's tone. "That was cold."

"I—I…wait! Dax, wait up."

Fat chance. He didn't even slow down, and was rounding the corner of the house when she grabbed his arm.

"Dax, will you please stop?"

He did, even though all he wanted was to hit the road and catch a ride. The sooner he did that, the sooner he could get his Harley fixed and make tracks out of Hummingbird Hollow. He'd clearly misread those mental pictures that had crashed his every prayer and meditation session for the past six weeks or so.

"I'm sorry." Toni's voice rang with regret. Was it real, or was she as good an actress as she was a singer? "You don't deserve that—not as one of my guests, and certainly not as someone who has shown himself kind and helpful. I…I apologize, Dax."

He said nothing for a moment, and then his lips twitched—with no warning and without his permission. Well, why not? He couldn't stay mad at her after what he had just witnessed. There was something special about Toni Littlebird…God-touched…even if she could be as prickly as a cactus.

Something was eating at her, and he'd give just about anything to know what it was.

He shook his head and tried to frown, even though his eyes were bound to be twinkling. Toni's sudden change of demeanor had turned on a fountain of pure delight inside him, and the eyes were, after all, the windows to the soul. Besides…dear Lord, she was beautiful! "It's not fair at all for you to use such a powerful arsenal against me."

"Arsenal?" The crease in her forehead deepened when she frowned. "I do not carry weapons."

Dax chuckled. "Oh, yes, you do. More than you know."

"Oh...well, uhm..." She bit down on her lip but didn't break eye contact. "Anyway, I'm leaving in a half hour or so. Can you be ready by then?" Her cheeks pinked, and she lowered her eyelashes. "I'd really like to make it up to you. Will you ride with me?"

He hesitated. "Are you sure? Because I can get a ride, believe me. I've ridden my thumb more than once."

"Well, your thumb can take a break today." She peeked at him beneath a protective curtain of long, dark eyelashes. "Ride with me. Please?"

Dax chuckled.

Woman, you're killin' me.

"I call shotgun."

"That won't be necessary. It's just the two of us."

"Well, okay...but it's fun to call it anyway, right?"

She laughed. "Yeah, I guess it is. So...shotgun! I get the driver's side."

Dax rolled his eyes.

"Careful with those things. They're not dice, you know. I'd sure hate to see them get stuck in place." She grinned. "Meet you out front in half an hour."

# 4

**DAX HAD NEVER LIVED IN** Arkansas. Still, as a resident of Missouri, its northern neighbor, he knew the state boasted many picturesque, small-town locations—and in terms of charm and historical authenticity, the little mountain town of Eureka Springs was unsurpassed.

Toni pointed out points of interest as they drove through, including a good many art galleries, and even a large old home-turned-writers' retreat.

Dax accompanied her inside a couple of establishments, then stood back and watched–astounded. Was this lovely, warm woman the same Toni Littlebird who'd met him with a hostile chill from the moment he arrived in Hummingbird Hollow? Then again, maybe that'd been for the best. Had she shown him this side of herself from the beginning, he might have lost his heart forever.

Merchants and business owners greeted Toni with broad smiles and welcoming hugs, as did Eureka Springs residents who milled in and out of the shops. Toni apparently knew almost everyone in the city. She asked about ailing friends and family members, expressed an interest in children who'd married and moved off to distant places, promised prayers for concerns big and small.

Everyone walked away smiling, each of them more relaxed and at ease than before their encounter with Toni. To Dax, who became more awed by the moment, it was as if she'd breathed some supernatural calm upon them, or maybe touched them with a special Native American blessing. Dax had never given much thought to such things, but now that he'd witnessed Toni's unique touch with birds and people, he couldn't discount the possibility. God gave spiritual gifts to His children—Dax knew that to be a fact. Who was to say the Father hadn't bestowed upon Toni the ability to calm troubled spirits—both avian and mankind—with a simple touch, or ease the grip of worry with a soft word of encouragement?

She bid the last friend a sweet goodbye, then turned toward Dax and blasted him with a thousand-watt smile that hit his heart like a bolt of pure, undiluted electricity. He managed a sideways grin in return.

He stood frozen as she approached, unable to remove his gaze from her face. Was this what it felt like to be turned to stone? Toni might or might not possess spiritual gifts, but her smile alone held the power to change lives. His would never be the same again.

After a moment of Dax's total inability to do anything but stare into her indeterminately colored eyes, Toni's fingertips brushed his, producing yet another electric tingle. This one shot from his fingertips to his shoulders—strong, but not unpleasant. He blinked and cast a quick look around. Surely he wasn't the only one who'd been hit by that burst of…whatever it was.

"You okay? You seem a little out of it."

"Yeah, uhm…well." Dax cleared his throat, surprised he'd even found his voice. "I guess I was kind of…out of it, for a moment or two." He forced a grin. "Hope I didn't do anything to embarrass you while I experienced that strange out of body experience."

One eyebrow rose high, the other dipped low. "No. You didn't embarrass me at all."

She stepped closer. Dax moved back, not sure his heart

could handle her lips being close enough to kiss.

"Dax." Toni took one more step and grabbed both of his shoulders before he could move away. "Seriously. Something's wrong. What's going on?"

He managed a chuckle, hoping it didn't sound more like the final croak of a dying frog. "I'm fine. Really. Don't worry about me." He reached for the bags hooked over one of her arms. "Here, I'll take those. Where to next?"

She fixed him under one last, penetrating stare. "Well, if you're sure..." Was that concern in her voice, or just wishful thinking on Dax's part? "I've done everything I need to do. Now let's go find something to make your horse feel better."

He laughed outright as he held the door open and she passed through in front of him. "My horse? Lady, I need a cure for a whole herd of horses."

"A herd?" Puzzlement drew her brows together. "I don't understand."

"Ninety-plus horses in that engine. That's a pretty strong herd, don'tcha think?"

"Ahh!" Her lips curved upward, bringing the sweetest little dimple out to play on her left cheek, and lighting a fire of enjoyment in those beautifully mysterious eyes.

Dax swallowed hard. Even his ninety-plus horses couldn't compare to the power in a smile like that.

He forced his gaze from her face, seeking any kind of anchor for his flailing emotions...and sucked in a sharp breath.

Toni stiffened when Dax's eyes widened and froze on something behind her.

"What?" She hissed the word, her heart pounding. "Dax, I should get you home. You're doing it again."

"No. No, I'm not. Just be still."

She frowned but did as he asked. After a few seconds, she smiled. "I hear it. Don't move. Just do that frozen-in-place thing again."

He nodded, his gaze fixed just behind her head.

Toni lifted her hand and placed a finger over her lips. Then she turned around.

"Hello, little one," she whispered.

The hummingbird hovered mere inches from her nose.

"You're having a feast today, aren't you? Just look at all the nectar around here, wrapped in lovely flower petals just for you. I hope you told Daddy God thank you for such a great big blessing."

The bird didn't dart away, so she held out a hand. After mere seconds of consideration, the little creature settled onto her palm.

"There, my darling. Rest for a moment before you return to your lavish meal." Without changing the tone of her voice, she addressed her companion. "Dax, can you glide?"

"Glide?" The word slid over her ears with silky overtones. How could a man with a voice as deep and rumbling and altogether wonderful as Dax's suddenly turn it into a luxurious auditory treat?

"Yes. Almost a waltz. Just glide a little closer and stand beside me."

Although highly tuned into her surroundings, she didn't hear so much as a whisper of rustling cloth or the scrape of shoes against the wood-plank sidewalk, and yet he appeared at her side. What a dancer the man must be...

"I want you to meet my friend. Isn't he lovely?"

"He is." A note of something almost reverent entered

Dax's voice. "He's stunning, and even after watching you with them in the garden this morning, I can't believe I'm seeing what I'm seeing right now."

He paused, but Toni said nothing. Somehow she knew he wasn't finished. Sure enough, after a few seconds he spoke again.

"And yet, even tucked into the palm of your hand like that, he doesn't hold a candle to you, Toni Littlebird. Not even close."

Toni tried to draw a breath but found she couldn't. She tried again. And again. At last, her lungs opened enough to allow a bit of air. Thank goodness! I doubt he'd find me quite so...whatever it is he meant by that comment...if I turned blue.

She bit back a giggle. Dax probably wouldn't find that attractive either, coming on the heels of such a compliment.

Why did it suddenly matter what he thought of her or her behavior? Besides, his words hadn't been exactly profound. She was behaving like a silly, lovestruck girl to react as she had.

But honesty compelled her to admit it hadn't been what he said that caused her breathless reaction. There'd been something underlying his words...something far deeper than the words themselves.

"Thank you! That's sweet of you to say." She dared a glance his way.

Big mistake. Not a glimmer of levity or teasing lit those gorgeous teal eyes. They held something that threatened to rob her once again of the ability to breathe.

"Not sweet at all." So softly spoken, and yet the words sent a tingle of something wonderful into her soul. "Just pure, undiluted truth."

Toni didn't know what to say, so she turned her attention

back to the hummingbird. "Goodbye, my darling. Go now, back to your big dinner." She blew a soft kiss into her hand and the hummer lifted up and away.

"Come. Let's get the miracle cure for your horses. Then I'll show you a little more of the area, if you'd like."

"I'd like. I'd like it a lot."

Dax required only moments inside the motorcycle shop—which he seemed surprised and delighted to find in Eureka Springs. When he returned to the car, he tossed a bag into the back seat, then reclaimed his place beside her. "Now let's go play, shall we?"

Toni grinned as she put the truck in gear and pulled back onto the road. "That we shall. And I know just where to take you first."

"Do you now?"

"Indeed I do."

"So are you going to let me in on the plan?"

She turned right onto Highway 62.

Dax cleared his throat. "Aren't we going the wrong way?"

"Nope."

"Okay. So is our destination a secret?"

"I guess not. I'm taking you to the Thorncrown Chapel first. Ever heard of it?"

When he didn't respond right away, she dared a quick glance away from the road—just in time to catch a strange little one-sided smile.

"What?" she demanded. "Did I say something funny?"

"No. Not at all. I'm sorry…just a passing thought. I've heard of the Thorncrown Chapel, but I have not seen it. Kind of odd, actually, considering I've lived within a few hours of it for such a long time."

"Why is that odd? Lots of people haven't seen it. Even those who've lived in Arkansas an entire lifetime. Not that it's been around absolutely forever, either. It went up in…nineteen eighty-six or so."

"Maybe…maybe a little earlier, I think. Nineteen eighty?" He shrugged. "You probably know more than I do about it. I should get out more, I guess."

"That's probably true of most people." She smiled. "You'll see it today. Better to be thankful you're seeing it now than to regret not seeing it sooner, right?"

"You're a wise woman, Littlebird."

She laughed. "You've called me by my last name a few times. Why not just Toni?"

"I kind of like Littlebird, if you don't mind, especially after seeing how you are with your little hummer pals. Strange that you'd have a name like yours and be so…so…" He paused, eyes narrowed in thought. "Sympatico with the tiniest birds in existence."

She nodded. "I think it's a God-thing. My mother also loved hummingbirds. Watching her with them was…uhm, it was…"

"I understand. I saw her daughter with them today, and I can't find the right words to define the experience either. It's a little surreal. Joyful and poignant at once. Powerful, actually."

"All of those things?" She affected a teasing tone, to still her own nerves. As an untamed, uncivilized biker who stank up her hollow and scared off her adored hummingbirds, Dax posed no threat to her heart. This Dax, on the other hand, stirred longings and emotions she wasn't sure how to handle.

*He's the one, daughter.*

Yes, well…

Toni pulled her bottom lip between her teeth and gave it a healthy nip. Nothing like a little pain to bring her to her senses.

"Aha! I've got it." Dax slapped his leg and grinned when

Toni stared. "Sorry, Littlebird. I just figured out your thing with those hummers. You're a hummingbird whisperer."

Toni blinked. A hummingbird whisperer?

"I'm not sure about that…"

"I am. I have no doubt whatsoever. But you're the real thing—not one of those phony folks who go 'round scamming folks out of their hard-earned money by making up things their pets supposedly are saying. You do this just between you and them…and it's a thing of intense beauty. This hard ol' heart of mine melted a little, watching you dance with those birds this morning."

Laughter bubbled up from somewhere deep inside her. "A couple of things. First, I've never heard the term 'hummingbird whisperer,' but I suppose that categorizes what I do as well as anything. But it's important to know that my little friends whisper to me as much as I do to them. Secondly, thank you for knowing I would never, ever use God's special gift as a way to hurt others in any way. And make no mistake…" She shot him a quick glance. "Whatever it is between me and the hummers, it is a God-given gift. I treasure that gift and cannot imagine being unable to have that time with them every day."

She drew a deep breath, unable to remember a time when she'd willingly spoken so many words at a time. Dax started to speak, and she held up a hand to stop him.

"Wait. One more thing. Your heart isn't hard. You have an amazing heart. It's strong, kind and compassionate. Never undervalue those qualities. Not for a moment."

Dax squirmed, clearly uncomfortable on the receiving end of such a compliment. "And what would make you think my heart's anything but granite, Littlebird…your hummingbirds?"

Toni smiled and pulled her vehicle into a slot. Then she

turned to face Dax and smiled. She laid aside all the friction between them since his arrival. Buried every hint of dislike. Stepped outside the shadow of fear under which she'd dwelt—though she'd refused to admit she was afraid since the moment Dax rode his herd of horses onto her property.

"No, Dax. The hummingbirds said nothing. I saw those things in your eyes."

She reached for the door on one side and touched her fingertips to his hand on the other. "Come on, cowboy. Let's check out this chapel."

Dax hauled in a breath—a deep one. Was it possible he experienced the same bolt of fire at her touch as the one that shot up her arm and lit a thousand flames in her heart?

He grinned, winked, and rested a loosely fisted hand against her cheek.

"That's Harley Cowboy to you, Littlebird. You sit right there."

Then, before she got a good grasp on what was happening, he was rounding the hood to open her door.

Just like a true gentleman cowboy.

# 5

AS THEY APPROACHED THE GLASS cathedral, a sense of awe took Toni in its grasp, as always when she visited this place.

Perhaps Dax experienced something similar, because he took gentle possession of her hand, without spewing humorous wisecracks, and with no explanation or apology. Not that Toni needed one. Her response was to curl her fingers around his, and to thrill at the simple contact.

She came here often—in times of great joy or sorrow, to celebrate victories, and to seek strength in hours of trial. She found it deeply stirring to pray, or simply clear her mind and enter a place of mental quiet, in a church that seemed to float within the sea of forested hills that surrounded it.

Dax pulled her to a stop just inside the beautiful glass building. She looked his way, only to be stunned by his captivated expression. He drank in the interior of the church as if his entire soul had yearned to be in the very place he stood at this moment.

"Could you…would you mind signing for me?" He waved a hand to indicate the podiums, one on each side of the room, topped by open guestbooks. "I want to…" He squeezed her hand and then released it as he walked away, his gaze darting from one side of the structure to the other. "…look around."

"Okay." Toni stared after him. Thorncrown Chapel fascinated all but the least sensitive of visitors, but Dax's reaction went beyond anything she'd seen. What lay behind his intense reaction? Perhaps he'd share what he was feeling when she caught up.

After scribbling both of their names in one of the guestbooks, she hurried to rejoin him, to perhaps experience the sanctuary through his eyes.

He stood near the windows behind the chancel. Both hands moved in a slow, gentle caress over one of the strong wooden trusses dividing huge panes of glass. Toni caught his muttered words and found herself ridiculously disappointed when he didn't sense her approach.

"Superb construction. All organic." He dropped to a squat and touched the floor. "Flagstone from the area...beautiful, and blends into the surroundings. Well done, Jones."

She fluctuated between interrupting his dialogue, which clearly wasn't intended as conversational material, and taking a seat where she could wait without interrupting his focus, but ultimately decided on the former. Whatever Dax was talking about, she wanted to be a part of it.

"Sounds a lot like you're talking to yourself. You know that's not considered a good sign, right?" She kept her tone of voice deliberately on the light side to counteract Dax's intense mood. "My Cherokee ancestors might say you've offended the Little People."

He stepped to her side, even smiled a little, but the rigidity in his stance proved impossible to overlook. His entire body thrummed—even though they weren't touching, the subtle vibration played on Toni's nerves. What could possibly be going on?

"Little people, yes...yes, of course." Dax shot her a quick, distracted smile, and then made a complete circle. Based on the rapid movements of his eyes, Toni decided he was trying to take in every detail of the chapel all at once.

She drew a deep breath, and then dared to touch his arm.

As she expected, he jerked as if a shotgun had gone off in the building. She sighed. "Okay, Dax, that's it. What's going on? You're...kind of scaring me, just a little."

He blinked, and then focused on her. For the first time since they'd arrived at the chapel, he seemed to really see her.

"I didn't mean to frighten you, Littlebird." He stepped close and, gently gripping both of her arms, pulled her close against his chest. "I'd never want to scare you. Please forgive me." Dax chuckled. "I've been somewhat weird all day, haven't I? Although I suppose my out-of-body experience back in town was nothing compared to this."

"You suppose correctly." Being held against his heart felt so right. Toni's heartbeat trip-hammered, and the reluctance with which she stepped free of his arms disturbed her. "Are you all right then?"

His answering grin soothed her uneasy spirit. Amused and fully aware, it was the grin she'd already come to recognize as the one most natural for him.

"As all right as any of today's youth when they meet their celebrity hero—or heroine, of course."

She frowned. "There's no one here except the two of us."

"The two of us and this incredible structure..." A note of reverence made its way into his voice. "It was designed by one of my heroes—E. Fay Jones. I can't believe I've never made the effort to visit, especially considering I live only hours from here."

Toni frowned. "Why is he your hero?"

"Because I've patterned my career after Jones's work— his craft, his ideology with respect to design. Jones is huge in my world."

"Your world. He was...Jones was a..." At last, a light went on in Toni's mind. "You're an architect!"

Dax smiled. "I'm no E. Fay Jones, but yes. As usual, you

didn't waste any time getting to the heart of the matter." He placed one hand on his waist, the other against the small of his back, and took a deep bow. "D. Dax Hendrick, Architect, at your service, m'lady."

Grinning, Toni placed both hands on her hips and sent him a narrow-eyed glance. "That's all well and good, D. Dax Hendrick—you being at my service and all. I'll find a way to take full advantage of that slip of the tongue, of course, but for now I've got only one, extremely burning question for you."

Dax's crooked grin melted another rather sizable chunk of her heart.

"Ask away, Lady Littlebird."

"What does the D stand for?"

Not a chance he was sharing his first name—at least not this soon. He'd be a bigger laughingstock than he'd been in her garden this morning. Maybe he could change the subject and sidetrack her curiosity.

"You don't want to know why a successful architect showed up on your doorstep on a Harley horse?"

"Well, yes, of course I do. Later. Right now, I want to know what the D—"

"Wouldn't you like to know why that same award-winning designer of beautiful buildings made an active effort to find Hummingbird Hollow?"

"Yes, but...wait. Are you saying the hollow isn't just a rest stop on your way to somewhere else? It's your destination?"

Dax hadn't meant to give that away until he knew the

'why's and wherefores' himself. But his heart said the time had come to reveal all. Maybe she already knew why he'd been sent here.

"Yep. It's where I was headed when I left my mountain."

Her eyes widened. "You have a mountain?"

"Well, I own a decent-sized piece of one."

Raven hair caressed her cheek when she shook her head.

"Well, I have to hand it to you, D. Dax Hendrick. You are a man of many layers." She smiled and reached out to cup his right cheek briefly in the palm of her hand. "I started to say 'many faces,' but my spirit tells me you show the same face wherever you are, and with whomever touches your life."

Dax blinked. The surprising compliment held tremendous meaning because it came from Toni, whom he believed spoke only what she believed to be truth.

"Thank you, Littlebird. That's kind of you to say."

She didn't smile. She didn't frown either. Her sober gaze traveled his face—giving him serious heart palpitations—and then found his. "One thing you should know about me from the start. I do not say nice things just to be kind. I say them if they are true. If not, I say nothing at all."

All Dax really heard was "from the start." What did she mean? From the start of what? Was it possible their relationship could become more than the 'professional' one her behavior had indicated the day they met?

He went with pretending she hadn't turned his whole world on its axis. "Then you and I have something in common. I don't believe in meaningless flattery either."

"Good." She smiled. "Now let's get back to the subject. Why did you come to Hummingbird Hollow?"

Why had he brought it up? Now she'd think he was off his rocker for sure. Still, he offered a grin that surely fell a good deal short of normal. "You won't believe me."

"You'd be surprised by the things I'll believe." A single dimple winked into sight when she smiled. "Talk to me."

She reached for his hand and started a slow stroll toward the door. "Are you finished here, for now? We can come again, but I kind of need to get back to the hollow. I didn't really plan to be gone so long."

"I do want to come again, but yes, certainly. Enough for today. Let's go."

Back in her vehicle, Toni wasted no time getting on the road. Dax hoped she might let slide the whole subject of his presence in her hollow. He should have known better.

The moment they left behind the slight traffic congestion at the chapel, she shot him a mischievous grin. "I haven't."

He frowned. "Haven't what?"

"I haven't forgotten what we were about to discuss. Sorry to dash your hopes."

He sighed. "So you're a mind reader too?"

"Not always. But your face is an open book. So, spill it. What brought you and your herd of horses into my world, D. Dax Hendrick?"

May as well give it up. She sure wouldn't.

"Visions."

Her eyes widened, and Dax derived some small measure of satisfaction from the response. She'd indicated a propensity to believe the unbelievable. Was it possible he'd already put that oh-so-confidently spoken claim to the test?

"Visions." She nodded. No trace of disbelief colored her tone. So perhaps that widening of her eyes had been nothing more than surprise. "That's not what I expected to hear. Tell me about them."

He hesitated, then went into confession mode.

"I heard you last night, playing your guitar and singing Amazing Grace. Something distinctly spiritual was taking place out there, Toni. I admit, I lay stretched out on the lawn for a long time after you went inside, just soaking in God's presence. It was more powerful than I've ever experienced, and almost overwhelmingly palpable. You brought Him there, you know…with your heart-praises, delivered in such a beautiful, sweet, sincere voice. Based on that—and your own statement when we met, that you serve Jesus Christ—I think I can assume you believe in prayer."

"Not only do I believe in it, I could not survive without it."

He reached across the seat to squeeze her hand. When she seemed content to leave her fingers nestled in his, he found himself pleased far beyond what the situation called for.

"Then that's something else we have in common, Littlebird. I believe in prayer, although I don't always pray in the traditional manner. Many times, my prayer time consists of meditation…focusing on God, on His blessings, on His presence in my surroundings—in nature, for instance."

"I understand. Remember my heritage, Dax. My ancestors were Native American—Cherokee, to be exact. While I don't adhere to all the old ways and teachings, meditation is one that I believe in very strongly."

Dax nodded. Of course she would understand meditation. Wasn't that pretty much the gist of what early Native American tribes had done in their smoke circles and vision quests?

"I'm glad, because during the past couple of months, every time I prayed or meditated, I experienced…" He chuckled. "I just realized I used the word 'visions' earlier. I've been hesitant to do so, preferring to call them 'prayer pictures.' But yes, they were visions. I kept seeing a lush, green hollow. I must've been shown a half dozen or more different settings, but somehow I knew they all lay within a single location."

"Hummingbird Hollow," she whispered.

"Hummingbird Hollow. I admit I'm a little hard-headed, but God finally got me to understand that I was supposed to find the place He'd shown me in my prayer pictures."

"So you just...what? Climbed on your horse and rode off, hoping Harley knew which way to point his nose?"

"Well, not exactly. I told God, 'I'll go if You say so. But I need some kind of direction.'" He slanted a look her way. "What do you think He showed me next?"

"He showed you a hummingbird."

Dax's head snapped in her direction. "How did you know that?"

She lifted one shoulder, and deftly swung the vehicle onto a narrow road. "Can you think of anything that would have made it easier to find me?"

Dax shook his head. "No, I guess I can't."

Within a few minutes, Toni took the Hummingbird Hollow exit...and then they were back at the B & B. He got out and joined her in front of the car, but his brain wasn't quite ready to move on.

She said 'find me.' Not Hummingbird Hollow. Me. Her. A simple error in phrasing? Or did it hold a deeper meaning?

He might be way off, but Dax's inclination leaned toward the latter. Toni Littlebird knew more about why he was here than she'd let on. Whatever it was, it was important.

# 6

**HE'D COME TO THE HOLLOW** for her.

Honesty compelled Toni to admit she'd known it from the first moment she met his blue-green gaze. Still, knowing he'd been sent to seek her out lent something definitive and solid to that knowledge.

Now the decision was hers. She'd always known he'd come along…Daddy God would send him. Now he was here. Daddy God had done His part, and the rest was up to her and Dax. Her heavenly Father might make His will known—even open the door for her to step through—but He'd also given her free will to make her own decisions, right or wrong.

After spending the day with Dax, she couldn't deny the attraction between them. No, it was more than an attraction. She'd heard of sparks flying between two people, but always considered it a metaphorical phrase. Maybe it was, for the most part, but between her and Dax the electricity was real, and powerful. Recalling the electric jolt that struck her heart when he first touched her hand, she once again struggled to draw air into her lungs.

She wasn't practiced at romance. While she'd dated now and then, there'd rarely been a second date with the same man. Her certainty that she'd "know him when she saw him" wouldn't allow her to instill false hope where none existed. If she didn't see that certain something in a man's eyes during the entire course of a first date, why keep seeing him?

As it turned out, no date had been required. She'd known

Dax from the instant she saw him.

She parked outside the garage and shot him a smile before opening her door. "Home, sweet crooked home."

Dax's jaw dropped. "Wh—what?"

Toni laughed. "Did you think I wasn't aware that my walls aren't quite straight, and that the floors give a little in certain places?" She allowed a brief beat of silence as she opened the trunk and reached for her packages.

Dax made no reply.

She slammed the trunk lid and looked up to find he hadn't moved a muscle. His chin hung almost to his chest—or at least, his dropped jaw left his mouth hanging open, which in turn sent the tip of his newly-trimmed beard almost as far down his chest as it had been when he first arrived. His horrified gaze was fixed on her.

Poor guy. She'd given him quite a shock.

Surely Daddy God would forgive her petty pleasure in watching him squirm…just for a moment. She grinned and shoved a couple of shopping bags into his arms, which closed around them in stiff, robotic reflex.

A sharp pinprick to her heart—all right, all right, Daddy God—warned her she'd gotten enough self-satisfaction from playing cat and mouse with Dax. Probably not a good idea to chase the man off, if they were meant to be more than friends. Much to her surprise—and to Someone else's certain pleasure—she was already halfway there, despite having been so sure that she couldn't and wouldn't love him.

She bit back a giggle. The problem might prove to be whether or not he could and would love her.

"No architect needed to spot the faults in my fortress, Dax. Normally I'd never mention the lack of symmetry…the crooked walls don't bother me, and I don't talk about them with my guests—they'll either love my home for what it is and return again, or they won't. But since you are who you are, I thought I'd acknowledge what, to you, is most likely an elephant in the room."

A flood of color rose from Dax's neck into his face. He closed his eyes and gave his head a slow shake. "I'm so sorry. I can't deny I noticed those things. I always do, wherever I am…it's the architect in me."

He shuffled all the bags into one arm and used the other one to take Toni's hand and draw her closer. Teal eyes did the same…capturing her gaze and refusing to let go.

"Dax, it's okay, I didn't mean to—"

"Shhhhh…let me finish."

She clamped her teeth down on her lip and nodded.

"The imperfections within your home…they don't matter, Littlebird. This place is what you've made it—a beautiful, warm, comfortable haven that invites visitors inside and makes them want to stay awhile, maybe even…" He cleared his throat, and the color in his cheeks deepened, but he plowed ahead. "…forever."

Talk about turning the tables. Toni snapped her jaw shut to keep it from taking the same path Dax's had only moments earlier.

Forever? Was he saying what she thought he was saying?

A low chuckle broke the frozen moment. "Please don't freak out. I have no intention of permanently corralling my loud, stinky horses in your hollow—or ensconcing myself in your home. I just wanted you to know how much I love it here in your 'crooked house.'"

She released her breath in a whoosh, then sucked it back in when he pulled her tight against his side and touched his lips to her cheek. He allowed them to linger just long enough to make her swoon, and then pulled away. Before she could think of the proper way to respond, he gave her hand a squeeze, walked inside and left her standing alone. The door swung shut behind him.

Toni braved the two steps to the car and leaned against it, thankful for the solid support of cold, hard steel.

Dax had kissed her cheek. Just her cheek. And as much as she'd like to believe it, the electric tingle radiating from every nerve in her body had nothing to do with the tickle of his whiskers against her skin.

It had everything to do with her overwhelming desire to turn her head and make the kiss a real one. Had Dax allowed his lips to linger even one second longer, she would've given in and done exactly that. In a scant two days' time, she'd come all the way from *I will never love him* to yearning for his kiss.

*No fair, Daddy God! I see what You're up to.*

She drew a deep breath and hauled her body up and away from the car. Her legs shook a little, but she ignored them, rebalanced the packages in her arms, and headed for the door through which Dax had disappeared and, for whatever reason, not returned.

Hiding out in the garage was not an option. Tomorrow morning, the weekend breakfast crowd would overfill the dining room and patio seating. She opened to the public only on Saturday mornings, when she served her locally famous Hummingbird Pancakes, drizzled with Cream Cheese Anglaise and topped with sliced bananas, chunked pineapple and toasted coconut. Jonathan cooked and served the delicious treats, but Toni got the batter ready and laid out the ingredients for the anglaise. Because her particular version of the recipe had been passed down from her Grandmother Littlebird, she wanted hers to be the hands that put it together.

She found Jonathan in the kitchen, already preparing for the next day's crowd. Dax was nowhere in sight.

"He's in his room."

Toni frowned, hoping to achieve a look of pure, innocent confusion. "Who?"

Jonathan didn't bother to answer, but his lopsided grin said plenty. He dove instead into an explanation. "He muttered something about putting on his cowboy duds and taking care of his horses. I got no idea what that bike dude was on about."

Toni tried to hold back a smile, but her lips would not be denied a twitch or two. Perhaps Jonathan wouldn't notice. The big guy would never let her live it down if he thought she'd so quickly fallen for the likes of Dax Hendrick.

"Hey, boss, did you remember the coconut syrup?"

"I did, although I'll never understand why anyone would prefer it to Cream Cheese Anglaise."

Jonathan laughed. "Have you even tried it? It's killer stuff, especially on your hummingbird pancakes."

"No, I have not, and I'm not likely—" Why was she always so unwilling to try new things? Dax wasn't, and he was far and away the most charming and fun person she knew.

When she broke off mid-sentence, the chef shot her a puzzled glance. "Toni?"

"Uhm...nothing. Just a brain glitch." She grinned. "If you recommend coconut syrup, I'll try it. Come breakfast time tomorrow, I'll pour the stuff on my pancakes."

Jonathan's eyes widened. "Who are you, and what have you done with my boss?"

"Oh, stop. I'm not that big a stick-in-the-mud, am I?"

"Well..."

They both burst out laughing. Toni loved that they could

be good friends and still maintain a professional relationship when a situation called for it. Still chuckling, she started unloading items from the bags she'd brought inside.

"I can't believe you two are having so much fun in here, and no one invited me to the party."

Toni dropped a can of crushed pineapples, narrowly missing her toes.

"Whoa, there. Didn't mean to cause a commotion." Dax bent to retrieve the can from beneath a stainless steel table.

"You okay, boss?" Jonathan touched her shoulder. His dark gaze searched hers without a hint of the levity from moments ago.

"I'm dandy, dude." Toni grinned at her own alliteration, determined to waylay his concern. He could be a big, protective bear if he thought she needed taking care of.

She accepted the dented can from Dax. "You startled me. I figured you'd already be dosing your horses with those meds you picked up in town."

"You are perceptive indeed, Littlebird." Dax's grin held a world of mischief—like a fun-loving little boy. "I had ta hustle myself out o' those city fixin's and into these here cowboy duds, don'tcha know? My horses, they get a little feisty now 'n then, and…well, ma'am, I shore didn't fancy lettin' them blasted animals mess up my Sunday-go-to-meetin' outfit. I'm a good sight smarter'n that." He tipped an invisible cowboy hat with one hand and stroked his beard with the other. "Yes, ma'am, yes indeed I am. Yes, indeed."

Laughter burst from Toni's lips despite her best efforts to dole out a convincing schoolmarm stare. "You're incorrigible, D. Dax Hendrick." She picked up a dish towel and shook it toward the door. "Be off with ya now, ya cowpoke. Them thar horses ain't a-waterin' themselves. Shoo! Out!"

He headed for the door with a comical bow-legged shuffle,

not once glancing at Jonathan, despite—or perhaps because of—the big man's laughter.

"I'll be takin' care o' those horses, woman, liken I always do. Just set yerself right here in this kitchen and don't be gally-vantin' off the property while I'm out and about. Ya hear me?"

"Oh, yes, sir…I do. I hear!"

"Hmmm. And jest what is it you hear, Littlebird?

Toni placed both hands on her hips, hiked one eyebrow and shook her head. "That's Miss Littlebird to you, cowpoke. Now be off with you…and don't be a-frightenin' my hummin'birds on your way to the horse stall." She giggled. "Or should I say 'stalled horse'?"

The chef let go a hearty laugh.

"That'll about do, ma'am. I've said my piece."

With that, Dax made his way to the door, trying hard to maintain the bow-legged shuffle and stomp out at the same time. Toni and Jonathan watched him go, sharing a moment of easy warmth and laughter.

When it was clear Dax wasn't going to pop back in with some silly comment straight out of a cheesy western show, she wiped her eyes and started collecting ingredients for her pancakes. Funny how a moment of silly banter could revive a flailing spirit.

She looked up to find Jonathan watching her, one dark eyebrow riding high on his forehead, his lips curved into an annoying smirk—which turned into a deep, knowing chuckle.

"Oh, hush, Chief Big Tiger." She dragged the name of an early Cherokee chief from somewhere in her memory as she plopped a big mixing bowl onto the counter. "And you really should pull that eyebrow down off the top of your head before it gets lost up there."

"Yes, boss." Jonathan turned back to whatever he'd been doing when she came in. He said nothing more, but the telltale hitch of his shoulders gave him away.

If she could get by without him, she'd send him out to help D. Dax with those infuriating horses.

Which reminded her…she still intended to find out the name behind that mysterious initial.

# 7

**DAX OWED JONATHAN. BIG TIME.** If not for the chef's casual mention that the B & B was open to the public for breakfast on Saturdays, Dax would most likely have been underdressed and overwhelmed when he arrived downstairs the next morning.

Always an early riser, he'd hoped to finish his own breakfast and be available to help Jon in the kitchen by the time the guests began to arrive. But upon swinging open the door to his suite, he was greeted by the rumble of a dozen or more different conversations all taking place at once. Intrigued, he stole downstairs, and then stood aghast, taking in the packed dining room. Through the open French doors, he glimpsed more people seated at tables and milling about on the back patio.

Pink and red filled every available space, and yet nothing seemed overdone or gaudy, just vibrant and fun. Tabletops bore scatterings of silver confetti hearts and small candies in red and pink wrappers. Petite bouquets arranged around taper candles formed simple, but pretty, centerpieces.

"Whoa!" Stopping short of a low whistle, he grinned and shook his head…until a burst of morning brain-power slapped him with the 'why' of this sudden color explosion.

Valentine's Day! Between last night and this morning, Inn the Hollow had transformed into a romance lovers' dream. Somewhere there must exist an army of Cupid-loving elves—probably red and pink ones.

Yet he hadn't given the holiday even the slightest thought. Until now, he'd not had much reason to worry about such things. He cast a quick glance around the room. Dare he hope one of the starry-eyed girls making goo-goo eyes across one of those Pepto Bismol-hued tables might trade a box of chocolates and a red rose for a crisp, new Benjamin Franklin?

Nah. Probably not.

"Did you say 'whoa'? I do believe you left your horses hidden away somewhere in the woods, D. Dax. They can't hear you."

His head whipped to the side, and for a second or two, he couldn't breathe.

A deep red dress with a subtle silver shimmer hugged Toni's slim form in all the right places—a gentle hug that epitomized grace, not one that threatened to choke the life from her body. The high, mandarin collar brought the bright color close enough to turn her eyes a translucent golden caramel and heightened the exotic effect of their slightly uptilted shape. From the white sandals on her feet to the red and white garland around her head, she looked amazing…and then some.

He grinned, hoping his appreciative head-to-toe visual scan wouldn't raise his hostess's hackles. "Good morning, Littlebird. You're a sight for early morning eyes."

"Thank you, sir—and a wonderful morning to you!" Her cheeks pinked, jump-starting his poor, unprepared heart…and then she smiled.

Dax swallowed a sigh and cast a silent prayer heavenward. *Hey, God…You're not forgetting I'm only human, are You? Lord, have mercy!*

"All I can say is, you've already made the trip down those stairs well worth the effort."

She shook her head. "You're quite the charmer, for a

Harley cowboy. Are you ready for breakfast?"

"I am, but I'm pretty sure you don't have an empty chair anywhere. I should go back upstairs and change into casual clothes. I can help in the kitchen and eat after the hordes have departed."

Toni's dark eyebrows shot upward. "Not a chance. You are my guest. We are busy this morning, but you have a special reservation."

"I do?"

She smiled and took his arm. "Come with me, sir."

Dax grinned and covered her hand with his. "I dare you to try and lose me any time soon."

Toni laughed. "I wouldn't think of it."

She led him out through the French doors. They wound through the tables, stopping a few times when guests called Toni's name. In each case, she offered a sweet smile and a few words of greeting, and then excused the two of them.

When at last they reached the lawn, Toni quickened her pace and giggled—a sweet, lilting, joyful melody that sent yet another powerful electric jolt through Dax's poor heart. "If we don't look like we have somewhere to be right away, we'll be eating breakfast at lunchtime."

Dax squeezed the hand she'd tucked through his arm. "We?"

"You don't miss a thing, do you? If you don't mind, I thought I'd steal you away for breakfast with me."

"I'm honored and delighted."

She lifted her gaze to his. Something wonderful danced deep in her eyes. "Here we are."

The garden gazebo, where he'd overheard her singing on his first night in the hollow, now boasted a drape of semi-sheer fabric—deep red, and pulled back only at the front to form an entrance. At the base of the steps, a hand-painted sign read

"Reserved," in a flowing script that Dax suspected might belong to Toni.

"Join me inside?" She indicated the opening in the fabric. Whatever held it back was well camouflaged by a swag of fresh pink and white flowers Dax couldn't identify. Gardening had never been his thing, but here in the hollow, he felt a budding interest taking root.

"Like I said, ma'am—you can't shake me now." He smiled. "The gazebo looks amazing."

"I'm glad you think so. Maybe you'll like what we've done inside, as well."

He followed her up the steps and through the gauze-framed entrance.

"Whoa!"

Toni's soft laughter flowed over his senses like warm honey. "Horse-speak again."

"Yeah, well...I couldn't find the right words. This is truly beautiful, Toni. Perfect" He chuckled. "I feel like—like David must've when they first brought him into the castle to play his harp for King Saul. Out of place, but oh-so-willing to get used to it."

Two of the cushioned benches that provided seating around the edges of the interior space now hugged a small, round table covered in white linen that pooled on the floor like a soft cloud. A three-branched candelabra graced its center. The drape of red fabric over the structure turned the space into a cozy hideaway that mimicked the semi-darkness of a romantic evening dinner. Dancing flames from the candles painted flickering patterns on two place settings that echoed the soft, robin's egg blue of the candles.

On the far side, filling the space usually occupied by the benches, a butler's cart held covered dishes, a selection of condiments, and yet another candelabrum.

"Shall we?" Toni's gaze seemed a bit uncertain.

"Of course. Sorry, Littlebird, don't mind me. I really am impressed with all of this."

He stepped forward to pull the bench back for her before claiming his own seat across the table. "Thank you for going to so much trouble. I didn't expect any special treatment."

"But you are special."

"Is that so?" He grinned, determined to keep things light, and not read too much into her kindness. "Says who?"

"Me. I say so."

"May I ask why?"

"Because...well, because...I—" She sighed. "I will tell you, I promise. But perhaps it'll be easier to talk over breakfast."

Off her seat in a flash, she glided to the serving cart and removed the lids from two covered dishes, revealing three stacks of pancakes and at least a dozen strips of thick bacon, fried crisp and brown, but not overdone.

Toni took Dax's plate. She overlapped four of the small cakes into a circle, added a small pile of sliced bananas and pineapple chunks in the center, and scattered toasted coconut over it all. A few slices of bacon went onto a smaller plate she must have snagged from somewhere within the storage drawers in the serving cart. Dax waited while she worked the same magic on her own plate, set two syrup pitchers on the table, and returned to her seat.

"Would you like to say grace, Dax?"

"I'd love to." He reached for her hands, and she placed them in his.

"Thank You, Father, for this wonderful breakfast with Toni. I'm grateful for this time in Hummingbird Hollow, and especially thankful that You allowed me to meet this beautiful woman who clearly loves You, and for the opportunity to spend a little time in her company. I'm a better man for the experience. Amen."

He squeezed her hands, released them, and picked up his fork. "And as a friend of mine likes to say at times like this, 'Amen! Dive in.'"

She laughed. "I agree with your friend, but I'm glad you spoke from your heart first. I know Daddy God appreciated it, and I certainly did." She cleared her throat and touched a finger to one of the syrup pitchers. "This is coconut syrup, which Jonathan swears is amazing with my pancakes. This one…" Her finger moved to the other pitcher. "This is warm cream cheese *anglaise*. It's my favorite." She wrinkled her nose and then grinned—a big, beautiful, utterly captivating grin that reached out and grabbed Dax's heart forever. "At least, I think it is. Jonathan made me promise to try the coconut syrup today, so I guess I don't really know just yet…but I can promise you the cream cheese *anglaise* is to die for."

"Well, then." Jonathan reached for that one. "I must try it." He poured the white glaze over a couple of his pancakes and then traded pitchers. "And I shall sample the coconut syrup as well. I must admit, I've never tried either of them on pancakes."

His fork sliced through the fluffy cakes, and a puff of heat rose around it, along with the most heavenly aroma. Was that…bananas? He opened his mouth to ask Toni, but she spoke first.

"I'm fairly certain you've never had pancakes quite like these, Dax. Go ahead. Taste and see."

He picked up a forkful off the cream cheese *anglaise* side of his plate, opened his mouth, and bit into the most incredible combination of flavors he'd ever tasted.

"Mmmm. Oh…my!" He spoke around the bite, then

closed his mouth, chewed and swallowed. "I didn't know anything this side of Heaven could taste like that. What are these? Did I hear you say you made them?"

Pleasure shone in her eyes, brightening them and pinking her cheeks as well.

"I did say that. My grandmother Littlebird used to make them, and then Mama did, as well—when she felt up to cooking."

A flash of sadness threatened to dim the light in her eyes. Dax held his breath until the smile returned.

"I make them now. Well, I put the ingredients together on Friday evenings. Jonathan puts them on the grill and gets them out to our guests."

"All I can say is, I don't care how much your guests pay for their Saturday morning breakfast, these pancakes are worth every single penny."

He dug into the coconut syrup covered pancakes, tasted, and nodded at Toni. "Good. Really, really good. I do prefer the cream cheese English, but the coconut has something special about it too."

Toni giggled. "*Anglaise*."

He cocked a brow, confused.

"Not English, Dax. Cream Cheese *Anglaise*. It's a French word."

"French for English. Right?"

"Well, yes, but—"

"But you like the sound of the French word better?" He grinned around another bite of bliss.

"No, it's just—" She stopped, tilted her head to the side, narrowed her eyes at Dax, and then grinned. "Yes. I guess I do like the French word better. It's so...pretty."

Dax laughed. "Well, I'll tell you what, Littlebird. Anytime you want to feed me these unbelievable pancakes—thank you,

Grandma Littlebird!—I'll call them whatever you want me to. Just keep 'em comin'!"

"Deal." Toni cut off a small bite and tasted it with a trickle of coconut syrup. Her eyes widened. "That's really good, isn't it?"

"Told'ja. But I do prefer the other one. I mean, come on…who doesn't like cream cheese?"

Toni smiled. "I'm glad we agree. But let's not talk about Hummingbird Pancakes and their various toppings all morning. I wanted to ask about—"

"Wait, wait." Dax held up a hand. "Before we move on, please tell me these heavenly pancakes do not include actual hummingbirds."

She laughed softly. "You don't really think I'd kill and cook my precious little friends."

"No, I do not. That's why I ate the pancakes." He grinned. "So where'd the name come from. Oh, never mind. You, of course. Because they're so sweet the hummingbirds like them too?"

"Hmm. Well, they are that sweet, but I'm afraid I can't take credit for the name. To be honest, I've not been able to find a really strong answer. There are several theories, but the one I find most likely says the cake originated in Jamaica, where one species—the swallow tail hummingbird—is the national symbol."

"Makes sense."

"Yes. But it's also said that it's called hummingbird cake because people hover around it like hummers around a feeder. And that the cake is so good it makes people hum with joy." Toni laughed. "All I know is, Arkansas folks seem to like it a lot."

"And I can see why." Dax laid his fork down and patted his stomach. "My horses will have a much heavier rider if I hang around here too long."

Her pleasure in the compliment shone in her eyes.

"Now that's settled, I'd like to ask you—"

"We're not back to 'what does the D stand for,' are we?"

Toni laughed outright. "Not yet, but I do intend to go there again."

"Let's give that one a little more time, shall we? About anything else, just ask away."

"I intend to. My curiosity is killing me. I hope you won't be angry, but I—"

She paused to nibble at her bottom lip. Dax closed his eyes and tried to picture something else…anything else, preferably something as far from tantalizing as possible.

"I Googled you."

His eyes flew open. "Wh—what? Why?"

"Because I want to know about you, and all you've told me is that you own a piece of a mountain, and that you're an architect. I saw pictures of some of your work online and…Dax, it's incredible. But then I found an article that said you'd resigned from the firm you worked for and just disappeared. Why would a successful architect leave it all behind and hide himself away in the woods?"

Dax sighed. She'd hit on a subject he avoided, but somehow, talking about it with her felt right.

"I was doing well. Really well. I got there on my own…clawed my way through the education process, working every job I could find to make it happen." He chuckled. "Folks probably thought I was a derelict during my university days. Between classes and sometimes three part-time jobs at night and on weekends, I didn't have a lot of time to sleep or eat. Looking at pictures of me back then is kind of scary. I looked strung out and anorexic. Becoming successful meant everything to me. No one knew how much, not even my mentor—the president of the company I worked for. He taught me a lot. We became good friends...or so I thought, right up until he stole my best design and took credit for it himself."

Toni gasped. "Oh, no!"

"Oh, yes. When I confronted him, he said he'd earned the right—that he'd made me successful. Without him, I'd still be waiting tables and drawing crayon houses."

"Dax...I'm so sorry."

"Don't be. When he threatened to fire me if I tried to claim the design, I saved him the trouble. Walked out of his office, climbed on my Harley, and started riding. I didn't stop until I spotted a 'For Sale' sign on a forty-acre lot several hours away and a good many feet higher in elevation."

"That's where you built your cabin?"

He grinned. "Did I call it a cabin?"

"Didn't you?" Toni frowned.

"If I did, I was downplaying the truth a bit. It's not a mansion by a long shot, but it's a good deal more convenient than a cabin."

"I see. But what about your job? What do you do now?"

"Ride my horses."

She rolled her eyes. "Without question. But how do make a living?"

"I do what I do best...design buildings. I do it on commission, from my home office, and I'm never without at least three jobs lined up at a time." He bit back a burst of laughter that might have been edged with bitterness. Despite the unbelievable success he'd found after 'disappearing' from society, talking about his old friend's deception still left a sour taste in his mouth.

Cool, slim fingers touched his and then slipped beneath them. He looked up to find Toni's eyes damp, her gaze soft.

"Sounds to me like Daddy God found a way to turn your friend's treachery into a good thing for you. If not for his despicable behavior, you might still be wearing a suit and tie eight hours a day, and designing according to specs dictated by others. Now you're doing things your way. I'd love to see some of your work since you left—" A charming double crease appeared between her eyebrows. "Where did you live before?"

"Jefferson City, Missouri. Now I'm northwest of Carthage. My property butts right up against the Missouri-Kansas border."

"Oh! Then you're not more than a couple hours or so from here."

"That's right."

"So I'm curious. How did you know which way to go after God showed you that hummingbird?"

"Well—much like you, Miss Littlebird—I am good friends with Google. I tried a variety of searches that included the word 'hummingbird,' and eventually found Hummingbird Hollow. No information was available about the hollow, but a map search showed me it was near Eureka Springs. And the rest, as they say, is history."

She shook her head. "I don't think so, Dax. I'm pretty sure 'the rest' is a good many tomorrows."

# 8

**TONI BIT BACK LAUGHTER AT** Dax's expression—it was kind of fun to watch him squirm. At last she took pity on the poor guy, released her lip from between her teeth and smiled.

"You're thinking I might not be quite sane, aren't you?" She tilted her head toward the gardens, where guests milled about after their pancake breakfasts, enjoying the antics of the hummingbirds. "Let's walk, shall we? Further into the hollow, perhaps…away from the throng?"

Dax, still wide-eyed, said nothing—but he stood, came around the table and offered her a hand. She raised herself off the bench. Dax tried to help, and clearly underestimated his own strength.

"Oh!" Toni managed only a quick shriek of surprise as she catapulted upward and straight into his arms.

Dax's chest rumbled with his deep, quiet laughter. "Pardon me, ma'am. Us cowpokes don't know much about much, when it comes to a purty lady. And you…" His voice deepened and lost all humor. He slipped a finger beneath her chin and lifted her face upward, forcing her to meet his gaze. "You are so beautiful!"

She gasped, and barely aware of her own actions, slid both hands up his chest to his shoulders. "Dax…I don't know—"

"Hush, Littlebird. Shhh…" He lowered his head so close to hers that his breath, laden with the sweet taste of hummingbird pancakes, fanned her lips and lit a fire in her soul. "Don't say anything, darlin'."

And then no distance remained between them. He touched his lips to hers, so gently, barely there, did-it-happen-or-not...almost like the kiss of a hummingbird. Even so, it reached deep, and wrapped around Toni's heart in a hug not meant to ever be released.

Moaning softly, she pressed closer. Dax gathered her in and deepened the kiss.

Fire raced over Toni's body, and blazed into her soul. She found herself unable to get close enough, and heard herself whimpering.

Dax moaned. He wrapped both hands around her arms and set her gently away.

She caught her breath and lifted her gaze to his, confused and a little hurt by the rejection. What she saw in his eyes stole the breath she'd only just found.

Desire. Raw, raging, barely bridled desire.

"Littlebird...honey, I want to hold you. I've never wanted anything so badly in my entire life. But look." He took her shoulders and turned her to face the fabric entrance. "You have guests. Lots of them. The last thing I'd ever want to do is be the reason they lose respect for you."

He slipped one arm around her shoulders and pulled her backward, just close enough for his lips to graze the back of her neck. "Or to show you any disrespect myself. You mentioned a walk. I think that's a great idea. A walk in the cool air."

Heat rose from Toni's neck and into her face in a huge, rolling wave. How could she have thrown herself at him like that? What must he think of her now?

Dax chuckled, took her hand and led her out of the gazebo. "Don't go thinking you know what's in my head. You're wrong, all right? Now, which way are we headed?"

Relieved to have a purpose, she led him around the gazebo, through the back part of the gardens, and onto a path that wound through a portion of wooded property. The shade beneath the trees provided cooler air that brushed her cheeks like a caress. Bless Dax for thinking of this!

They walked in silence through the woods, while Toni fought back tears. That kiss! Who knew she had such passion within her? How could she ever look at Dax again?

"Littlebird." Dax pulled her to a stop by swinging her in a circle and back into his arms. "Whatever you're thinking, stop. I won't let you lessen the beauty of our first kiss by coloring it in ugly shades of shame. It was a beautiful moment—one I will never forget. And I won't let you forget it either. Not ever."

She dared a peek up and past his beard. As if she stood outside her body as an observer, she watched her finger reach out and stroke his lips. Dax gave the naughty digit a gentle nibble, sending zaps and zings of powerful emotion throughout Toni's body.

Despite the electric shower—which was in no way unpleasant—she reclaimed her finger ever so slowly. "Never? How will you make me remember? This is my home, here in Hummingbird Hollow with my hummers. You and your herd of horses live on a 'respectable piece' of some mountain in Missouri."

"Living arrangements can be changed. Guess we'll have to talk to God about that. But even if we lived a whole world apart, I could never forget how your lips felt against mine. That kiss…it wrapped itself around my heart, Littlebird. Forever. I—" He paused, and shot her a sheepish glance, but still he continued. "I felt it happen."

Her eyes couldn't possibly be as wide as they felt. "You too?" She managed only the merest whisper.

"I did. And I knew you did. There was a tug on my heart when that eternal embrace tightened around yours."

Toni studied his gaze for any sign of insincerity, and found none. She drew a deep breath, nodded once, and stepped back. She'd never get through her story if she remained in his arms.

Dax took the hand she offered, and she set off at a much brisker pace. "I have something to tell you, D. Dax Hendrick. Let's find a place to talk. Until then, please don't say anything else. I need to calm my spirit."

"I think I can handle that. Hey, you don't suppose that little guy over there is trying to tell you something, do you?"

Toni followed his gaze. Just ahead of them, a beautiful albino hummingbird hovered at eye-level.

"Diamond!" Toni smiled. "What are you doing out here, little one?"

The hummer zoomed toward them, landed on her shoulder, and edged itself close to her ear. A stream of soft chips and chirps followed.

"Why, thank you, sweet girl. Lead the way."

Diamond lifted up and away. She streaked through the woods like a flash, and then circled back to put herself once again in their line of sight.

"I gather she's taking us somewhere?" Dax hadn't spoken during Toni's interlude with the bird, and he did so now with quiet respect.

Toni squeezed his hand and shot him a quick smile. "She says it's a secret place. I get the feeling she's sharing it only because she knows we're in love."

Dax hoped his expression didn't reflect how much her words

shocked him. He hoped in vain, which became all too apparent when Toni laughed—the first lighthearted reaction she'd displayed since he kissed her.

"Don't take me so seriously, cowboy!"

He shook his head. "How do you get from scary serious to…scary playful in a heartbeat? And are you saying you didn't mean what you said?"

"Nope." She ducked under a low branch, and Dax followed suit barely in time to avoid butting his head against it. The moment he stood upright again, Toni's amused glance met his. "But I'm not saying I did, either."

"So, what then? I'm supposed to figure it out? Danged if women aren't the orneriest creatures in existence!"

"Oh, you think so, Harley cowboy? Want me to read you a list of your less admirable moments?"

"Uhm…nope. I guess we both have a little rambunctiousness in us."

"Handsome and wise. Where's Diamond?"

The hummingbird darted into sight, as if Toni's question had carried across the small clearing in which they now stood.

"There you are, my darling. You might slow down a little. We humans don't have the option of moving with anything remotely close to your kind of grace."

The bird eased off whatever accelerator she used to increase and decrease her natural speed. She flew around a large oak, and the moment Toni and Dax caught up, she set off again. This time, she disappeared over a small rise.

"You sure she's leading us somewhere?" Dax didn't want to sound doubtful, but communicating with hummingbirds wasn't exactly his field of expertise—nor even something he'd thought possible until he met Toni.

"Bite your tongue!" Toni laughed as they reached the top of the rise, and then went quiet when they looked down the other side. "Where's Diamond?"

He scanned the area and shook his head. Unless the hummingbird wanted to be found, she'd be difficult to spot amongst the lush spread of trees and vegetation. "I don't see her."

"She'll show herself in a moment."

The words were barely spoken when the hummer appeared on the south side of the clearing. She hovered above an oversized thicket of bushes growing against the slope of a hill. Honeysuckle vines had made themselves at home amongst the leaves and branches. Its sweet fragrance drifted on a light breeze.

Diamond flew in agitated circles over the lush growth, and then disappeared again—behind the vegetation.

As they drew closer, Toni gasped. "Is that a—?"

"Yep. It's a cave," Dax supplied.

Diamond hovered near the dark entrance.

"How did I not know about this?" Toni shook her head, only half believing what she saw. "Well, D. Dax, it appears we're going inside."

"Looks that way. You ready for this?"

"I don't know, to be honest, but…ready or not, here we go."

She took three steps before Dax stopped her by tugging on the hand he still held.

"Uhm, I understand you're a modern, independent woman. You're used to doing things for yourself. But I'm an old-fashioned cowboy at heart, ma'am. I'd really prefer to go in that black hole ahead of you, if you don't mind."

Toni fluttered her eyelashes and spoke in an exaggerated southern drawl. "Well, if you aren't just a big, brave *gentleman.* By all means, sir, go right on in that scary cave and use your cowboy powers against any…" She paused and tilted her head to the side, eyes narrowed as if in deep thought. "*Unsavory* creatures in there—human or otherwise, if you know what I mean." Her eyes widened. She gave her eyelashes another playful flutter, grinned and waved an arm toward the cave. "You first, cowboy."

"Thank you, Miss Arkansas. You stay out here until my pretty face shows up again."

"Right you are." She pointed a finger at her toes. "These feet won't budge so much as an inch."

"That's the way I like it, Miss Littlebird." He puffed out his chest, straightened his shoulders, stuck his nose in the air and strutted toward the cave. "Here I go. Braving the unknown. Risking both heart and mind—all for a woman who doesn't like me much, and downright detests my faithful Harley horse."

Toni's laughter followed him through the narrow opening in the hillside.

As she'd promised, Toni remained where she stood. A minute passed, and then another.

"Dax?"

He didn't respond.

Every instinct told her to hurry inside and check on him. But she'd promised… With a sigh, she determined to allow him two more minutes before going after him.

She counted it down, and when the second "Sixty, one thousand" rolled around, she stiffened her shoulders and took a step toward the cave. Maybe the cowboy needed to be saved by the lady.

"Littlebird!" Dax appeared in the entrance. "Get in here,

darlin'. You've got to see this."

As soon as she reached his side, he took her hand. "Be as quiet as possible."

She couldn't help smiling. Even in the dim cave, his blue-green eyes shone wide and bright. Excitement burst from every pore in an almost visible explosion that reached out and touched Toni as well. A slight tremor in her fingers testified to its impact.

They stood inside a small, low cave. Nothing spectacular. Dax led her to the opposite side of the space and around a curve that hadn't been visible from the entrance. Toni gasped when the slight turn placed them in a dark tunnel.

She heard the jingle of metal against metal, and a tiny beam of light pierced the darkness.

"Where'd that come from?"

"On my keychain. First time I've ever had to use it. Sure am glad it works."

Their whispered conversation seemed to carry and create vague echoes.

"What am I supposed to be seeing?"

"It's around a bend, straight ahead. Shhh!"

Toni giggled. She couldn't help it. Something about the fervor within Dax's 'shush' tickled her.

They followed the tunnel a short distance. Based on the downward slope, they were going further underground. She didn't realize how nervous she'd grown until they rounded the curve Dax had indicated.

Her growing anxiety disappeared in an instant.

Smooth, shiny rock walls formed a round room. She blinked, surprised by the lack of darkness.

Dax pointed overhead, where sunlight poured through a fissure in the rock surround.

Toni barely drew breath as her gaze followed the glorious

rays of heavenly sunshine. Then she hauled in a lungful of air and nearly fell to her knees. Surely God had created the natural skylight to showcase the scene below.

# 9

**A LITERAL CLOUD OF HUMMINGBIRDS** whizzed and darted and soared around a small geyser that spewed several feet into the air.

"An underground spring!" Toni breathed the words on an exhale. "There's a network of them in the area. They gave Eureka Springs its name. This must be a part of that grid."

Dax nodded. "Probably, but whatever its source, I think your friends like it." He pulled off a light jacket and spread it on a rock shelf that ran halfway around the cavern, at a height perfect for seating. "Have a seat. The view's unbeatable."

When she was comfortable, he took the space next to her and drew her close against his side.

"Have you ever seen anything like this? There must be hundreds of them."

Toni shook her head. Even in her gardens, where twenty-five to forty or so hummingbirds darted about at any given time, she'd never witnessed a sight like this.

At least a hundred tiny birds—maybe twice as many—danced around the gentle geyser. They'd dip under the spray and then dart off, where the rapid beat of little wings no doubt dried the moisture in an instant.

"Look over there."

Toni followed Dax's pointing finger and smiled. A narrow crack in the surrounding rock fed water from the spring into a slight indentation. The anomaly formed a shallow pool off the stream. Here, the water moved enough to prevent stagnation but not swiftly enough to present a danger to the tiny creatures who'd made it their haven. It created a perfect bird bath. Hummers dipped and dived. Some hunkered right down in the pool, where they preened themselves in the moisture.

"So many of them," Dax whispered. "And look at all the colors."

Toni nodded. "I've done a tremendous amount of research on hummingbirds. Some of these little guys aren't even supposed to be in this part of the world, much less here in Arkansas."

"And in your hollow, specifically?"

"Right. I've decided they are God's gift to me, perhaps because He knows how much I love them, how I learn from them."

Dax shot her a quizzical glance. "What have they taught you?"

"Many things. They are not deterred by limitations—being small, for instance. They're efficient and flexible. Brave, too—they'll defy much larger birds to protect what they perceive as their own territory. Hummingbirds are rarely still...always busy at work or play." She chuckled and butted Dax's shoulder with her own. "For the males, it's mostly play. The females do all the labor of building nests and caring for the babies, while the males serve only as breeders. Once they impregnate a female, they're off to the next one. My little friends, despite so many good qualities, do not mate for life...or even for a whole day at a time."

"What a life!" Dax grinned, but sobered right away. "Seriously, that's not the kind of life I would ever want."

Toni bit back a smile that would probably be far too radiant and narrowed her eyes instead. "Flitting from one relationship to another doesn't appeal to you in the least?"

"Never been my style. Never will be." He turned on the

hard rock bench to face her, and pulled her close. "Now that I've found my Littlebird, I'll never want another woman. Ever."

"How can you know that?" She nuzzled her forehead against his chin.

"You don't know it?"

"Oh, yes…I do, but I have a reason."

"Care to share?"

Toni hesitated. Should she tell him why he'd been so easy to fall in love with, despite her initial dislike of him and his bike?

Dax lifted her chin with a finger and dropped a quick kiss on her lips. "Talk to me."

"All right, I will tell you. But if I see so much as an instant of disbelief in your eyes…"

"You won't. I've already learned to keep an open mind around you."

She studied his face, searching for…what? Duplicity? Dax wasn't capable of such a thing. Disbelief? She didn't see that either. In his steady gaze, she found only sincerity, honesty and…something else. Something that engulfed her in a wave of longing and left her weak.

"OK. Here goes." Unwilling to reveal the strength of his effect on her, she managed a smile, only to find her lips atremble. She sighed and plunged into her story. "I was very young—maybe seven or eight—when my mother told me about the day I was born." She chuckled. "Her name was Gentle Willow. She was beautiful. Gentle, just as her name indicated, and quiet—but when she spoke, she spoke from a place of wisdom. I loved her so much."

"I know she's proud of you now." Dax brushed his lips over hers—a sweet, almost reverent kiss that wielded tremendous power. Strength and determination flowed from his soul to hers.

She could do this.

"I hope so." She smiled. "Anyway, Mother named me LiTonya. It means 'hummingbird darting.' She said that, during her entire labor and delivery, a hummingbird kept watch from the window of the room where I was born. He dashed off every now and then to feed, but always returned to hold vigil at the window. After I arrived, the little creature nestled on an outside ledge until I was clean, fed, and sleeping soundly. Curious to see what the little guy would do, my mother asked the midwife to open the window. Within moments, he flew inside and settled on the edge of my crib. He stayed there a few minutes, and then glided across the room and back outside.

"According to my mother, the hummingbird is my 'spirit animal.'" She smiled. "I prefer to believe God is my spirit guide. He sends the birds to me for inspiration and joy. They speak, you know—not in words, exactly, but I understand their language, and they seem to understand mine."

Dax nodded. "That's easy enough to see."

She snuggled into his embrace. "Mother also told me about you, Dax."

He stiffened, and then gently set her far enough away to meet her eyes. "About…me? How is that even possible?"

"All things are possible."

"Wh—what did she say?"

"That God had created me for someone very special, and him for me. I asked how I would know, when the time came, whether a man was the special one Daddy God meant for me to spend my life with. 'When you meet him,' my mother said, 'you will know him to be the one.'" She pulled in a deep breath and continued. "She also said that when I knew him, I would love him."

Dax expelled a short, hard breath. "I'd say Gentle Willow missed that by a country mile or so."

"No, Dax. She did not. The day you arrived, when I first looked into your eyes and peered through all the colors of the ocean...I knew you were the man my mother had spoken of."

"But you didn't love me." Dax spoke with firm insistence.

"I didn't know that I did. I told Daddy God that I would never love you, even though being in your arms stole my breath and awakened my very soul." She looked up and stroked a hand over his cheek. "I'd say He's laughing out loud right now."

"You think so?" He pulled her close and brushed her lips again...a gentle slide from one side to the other. "That may well be true, darlin', but I don't think 'Daddy God' could possibly be any happier than I am at this very moment."

"And why is that?"

"Because I love you too, my beautiful hummingbird whisperer."

He kissed her temple, slid his lips slowly down the curve of her cheek and to her chin.

Toni whimpered again, every nerve on fire. "Dax..."

"Shhh." He touched a finger to her lips and trailed it over her chin and to her throat. When she thought she couldn't draw another breath, long fingers splayed across the back of her neck and drew her face closer to his. His mouth teased at the corner of hers, and then slid across their length to repeat the tantalizing lip dance on the other side.

"Dax...please..."

He didn't ask what or why or when. He covered her lips with his own. Toni breathed a silent sigh and slipped her arms up and around his neck. She nestled closer, desperate to become one with him. Surely there was a way...

After a moment, Dax gently set her back and stood,

breathing hard. "Time to go, darlin'." He took her hand and pulled her upright, then kissed her forehead. "I have a feeling we'll visit this little slice of paradise many, many times. But right now, we need an audience."

"I don't understand." Her lips felt tender, tingly and wonderful.

"Littlebird, it's time to go, while I still can." He met and held her gaze. "Let's do this thing God's way, shall we?"

Heat rushed into her cheeks as his meaning became clear.

"Oh, Dax…" Both hands flew to her cheeks.

He chuckled. "You did nothing wrong. Let's keep it that way."

She nodded and turned for a moment to watch the hummingbirds at play. Diamond darted over and hovered a foot or so in front of her until Toni held out a hand. The little bird perched on one finger.

"Thank you for sharing this beautiful place with us, precious girl. I can see it's special to you and your friends. Dax and I will never reveal your secret hideaway to others."

The bird lifted up and onto Toni's shoulder, where it nuzzled a tiny head against her hair. Then it shot off toward the geyser in a blur of white wings.

They spent the entire day together and discussed everything from their favorite elementary school teachers to the worst days in each of their lives. Toni showed him all her favorite spots in the hollow, including the one on which she'd long dreamed of building a small chapel. He told her about his childhood in Jacksonville, where his parents still lived. They discovered tons of shared interests, and a few topics on which they laughingly agreed to disagree.

After dinner, huge mugs of hot chocolate in hand, they cuddled beside fireplace, staring into the flames, content to be together.

Dax broke the silence with a request. "Sing for me, Littlebird." He pointed his chin toward her guitar, propped on its stand next to the hearth.

She blushed. "I don't think I can."

"I know you can. Remember, I've already heard you, and I think your voice is amazing, so there's no need to be nervous."

"Well…"

"I really, *really* want to hear you sing."

Toni wanted nothing more than to stay right where she was forever—snuggled close to him, watching the fire and thinking beautiful thoughts. But he'd asked her to sing, so she picked up her guitar, closed her eyes and strummed a few random notes.

Quietly at first, and then with increasing confidence, she sang a Cherokee healing song. Dax watched her, and that little something in his gaze—still there, constant and steady— spoke to her heart as clearly as did the voice of the hummingbirds in her gardens.

When she finished, he stood, took her in his arms and gave her one last slow, thoroughly soul-shaking good night kiss. Then he pulled away and touched a finger to the tip of her nose.

"As much I'd love to sit here and hold you until the fire dies all the way down, I have some work to do before I get any sleep. I guess…" He sighed and stroked the same finger along her cheek. "I have to get busy."

"I understand. See you in the morning."

She watched him climb the stairs before making her

rounds to lock doors and turn off lights. When she finally crawled into bed and switched the lamp off, she was certain she'd lie awake all night, thinking about Dax—his beautiful, ocean-colored eyes…firm, well-defined lips…even the beard she'd disliked at first had become part of his charm. Instead, she fell asleep almost at once, and awakened refreshed and eager to see what the new day would bring.

Her meditation time in the garden proved less than satisfactory, as her mind insisted on replaying every moment of the previous day. The hummers seemed to sense her disquiet. They clustered around her, chipping and chirping a calming mantra.

Back inside, Dax was nowhere in sight, but she found Jonathan in the kitchen, humming a lively tune while dropping eggs into a skillet sizzling with hot butter.

"Morning!" She reached for a plate. "Seems quiet, after yesterday's crowd, doesn't it?"

"Well, yes, but I can't say I'm complaining."

Toni laughed. "I can understand why. You did an amazing job, as always, Jonathan." Heat crept into her cheeks. "I appreciate having someone I can depend on, even when I desert the place like I did yesterday."

Jonathan shook his head. "I was glad to see you take some time for yourself. And Dax is a good guy. You have my approval—I mean, you know, in case that matters."

"Of course it does. I value your opinion, Jonathan. You don't volunteer it often, but when you do, it's almost always exactly right."

"I don't know about all that, boss, but thanks."

"Speaking of Dax…has he had breakfast yet?"

"No, I haven't seen him this morning." Jonathan paused, frowning. "Come to think of it, that's unusual. He's always the early bird."

"Well, he did say he had some work to do last night. He may have been up until who knows when."

"Well, what about you? Can I fix you an omelet, or anything else you'd like?"

"I'll wait a few minutes. I'm sure Dax will be downstairs soon."

She busied herself dusting and picking up bits of clutter looked over by the cleaning staff after yesterday's holiday breakfast, and then on the patio, straightening chairs and watering plants.

When Dax still hadn't made an appearance, she grew concerned and took herself back to the kitchen.

"Jonathan, Dax still hasn't come downstairs. Would you…would you mind checking on him, please? I'm not sure it would be appropriate for me—"

"No." Jonathan glanced at the clock and peeled off his apron. "You're right, boss. I'll do it."

Toni waited at the bottom of the stairs. Her heart sank when Jonathan reappeared and shook his head.

"No answer. Is his bike here?"

"Oh! I didn't even think to check."

"Stay here. I'll do it."

He zoomed out the door. Dax's Harley had been repaired the day they went to Eureka Springs, but he'd left it parked in the shed. Toni paced the floor, casting a glance upstairs every thirty seconds or so, until the chef returned, concern etched into his features.

"His bike's gone, Toni."

Her stomach lurched, and she drew a deep, steadying breath. No sense drawing wild conclusions about his absence. He loved her. She knew it. He wouldn't just up and disappear like this without a good reason.

Would he?

"OK, I'm going in." She managed a shaky grin. "You've done enough, Jonathan. Thank you. You can get back to what you were doing."

"Boss…are you sure?"

"Absolutely." With a smile, she grabbed the spare key from behind the counter. Determined not to put her uncertainty on display, she took the stairs at a brisk stride.

Once out of sight of the lower floor, she stopped trying to hide her fear. She grasped the doorknob, and then leaned her forehead against the door.

"Daddy God? You sent Dax here, didn't You? He's the one. I can't have been that far off."

Perhaps Dax wasn't so certain *she* was the one for him. Maybe he'd lost his nerve after coming upstairs last night. Come to think of it, his decision to leave their cozy space in front of the fireplace to do some work had certainly come out of the blue.

Lifting her chin, she turned the key, pushed the door open. The bed was made. Had he even slept in it?

When a tingle started in her fingers, she realized she was hyperventilating a little and forced herself to breathe normally. She couldn't let this…whatever it was…destroy her.

Another step into the room, and she spotted an envelope on the desk under the window. Only four steps away, but each one felt a mile long, as though she moved in slow motion.

She lifted the desk lamp, which Dax had used as a paperweight, and picked up the proof of his departure. Pain lanced her heart when she recognized the neat print, with a hummingbird sketch on each end of the single word:

*Littlebird*

Her fingers trembled, making it difficult to open the envelope. When her legs joined the action, she sat and opened the drawer in search of a letter opener.

A sketchpad lay inside the shallow drawer space. Toni laid the envelope aside, pulled out the drawing tablet, and started turning pages.

Was he designing some weird, modernistic church? No, it was too small. What in the world was he working on?

Her stomach lurched when she spotted the tiny print in the right-hand corner. "Littlebird's Chapel."

Horrified, she skimmed through page after page of drawings—all ultra-modern, with sleek, unlovely lines and no heart...no character. By the time she reached the last page, which Dax hadn't bothered to finish, she was glad she hadn't eaten, given the unsettled state of her tummy. Her chest ached as if a giant hand squeezed it in a cruel, unrelenting grip—a physical manifestation of the excruciating pain in her heart. Even her spirit wilted beneath a heavy cloak of defeat and disappointment.

Toni crumpled to the floor, crushed by an unbearable weight of sorrow, and curled her body around itself. Silent tears streaked her face. She let them fall unrestrained.

*Oh, Dax...Dax!*

All the beautiful moments, all the spine-tingling kisses and sweet words had clearly meant nothing more than a pleasant interlude to him. If he had imagined, even for an instant, that she'd allow any of these skillfully designed but utterly soulless plans to be erected in Hummingbird Hollow, then He knew nothing about her. Why, her ancestors would come up out of their graves!

How could she have been so horribly wrong?

*Daddy God...why?*

Perhaps He was busy with some other fool who thought

they knew the mind of God, because no answer came in the hour of her desperate need. No comfort. No peace.

Some time later, she pulled in a deep breath that still hitched with the remnants of her sorrow. She uncurled her stiff body and stood to her feet, suddenly possessed of an icy calm.

Back at the desk, she dropped the unopened envelope in a nearby trash container. No point in looking inside. This empty room said more than she wanted to know.

She shoved the sketchpad back into the drawer. Maybe someday she'd pull it out and have someone send it to the guest who'd left it behind. For now, she'd leave it where it was...locked away in darkness, along with her heart and her memories of a pleasant, laughing, handsome man who wasn't "the one."

# 10

**DAX ROARED PAST EUREKA SPRINGS** on his "Harley horse." Four agonizingly long days had dragged by since he stole out of Inn the Hollow somewhere around dawn, headed for his mountain hideaway.

While Toni sang that last evening, he'd watched the firelight dance over her face and hair. Her beauty stole his breath and every sane thought in his head. He wanted this woman by his side for a lifetime—*needed* her more than he needed the breath she took away. He'd be happy to spend every moment of the rest of his life making her just as breathless.

That's when inspiration struck. He could get started on that goal right now, by designing and building her dream chapel. With ideas bouncing around in his head like Mexican jumping beans, he excused himself and headed upstairs.

In his room, he grabbed the cheap sketchpad that went everywhere with him, in case of just this kind of unexpected inspiration. His fingers flew as he sketched out a dozen or so basic layouts. They were good, he knew they were. But they weren't right—not for Toni, not for Hummingbird Hollow.

Frustrated, he set the sketchpad aside, dropped to the floor and crossed his legs. Maybe clearing his mind would help.

Fifteen minutes later, his eyes flew open. Grinning, Dax jumped up and started tossing things into his duffel bag.

"Thank You, Lord! Why is it that I don't come to You first every time?"

He'd *seen* the chapel, and it was perfect. But he couldn't show it to Toni in a simple sketchpad drawing. He needed to be in his office, in his familiar workplace, surrounded by all the tools of his profession, so he could create a presentation that would insure she saw it as clearly as he had.

He couldn't wait for morning. Toni would understand…he'd leave a note, along with a check to hold his room until the end of the month, in case it took him that long to get back—which it wouldn't. A few hours of riding time, a few days to perfect his presentation. With any luck, he'd be back before a full week passed, with a belated, but truly breathtaking, Valentine's gift.

Despite his excitement, a bit of worry niggled at the back of his mind. He'd tried to reach Toni on her cell phone several times, but every call went straight to voicemail. He'd called the landline twice. Meli answered both times, and politely informed him that "Ms. Littlebird" was unavailable. He'd left messages, but never received a return call.

Something felt wrong, but he was probably worrying for no reason. Surely Jonathan would have let him know if Toni was ill or otherwise indisposed.

Dismissing the vague disquiet in his soul, Dax took the turnoff to Hummingbird Hollow, grinning like an idiot. Three minutes, and she'd be in his arms—and this time she'd be happy to see him.

He parked in the same place he'd parked his slightly crippled Harley on his first unwelcomed arrival, grabbed his portfolio from the saddlebag and rushed inside, expecting Toni to meet him at the door and catapult into his arms, like before…but with a great deal more warmth.

Instead, she stood straight and tall, and cold as a Pocahontas statue, behind the reception counter.

"Littlebird…" Dax breathed her name and opened his

arms.

"What are you doing here, Mr. Hendrick? I suggest you get back on your horse and keep riding. There's no room available at Inn the Hollow. Not for you."

The compelling excitement on his face vanished in a slow fade, replaced by a shattered expression that went soul deep.

It was almost Toni's undoing. She deliberately called to mind his hasty departure after a day of supposed bliss. The beautifully drawn, completely *wrong* sketches she'd found in his desk. The days of agonizing loss that followed. Only those painful memories kept her from flying into his arms.

After a tense moment loaded with unbearable emotion, Dax managed a sick, shaky smile.

"Littlebird? You're kidding, right? You need some practice on what's considered funny and what's just...*not*, you know?"

"That's *Ms.* Littlebird to you. I believe you left a couple of..." The image of his sketchbook in the desk came to mind in full, ugly detail. "Belongings. They're still upstairs. I'd appreciate you clearing them out immediately, so I can book the room."

His ocean-colored gaze held hers, after a slow journey over her face. Toni ignored the tiny lightning bolts that shot into her bloodstream and heated her from the inside out.

His handsome face—always so warm and open—became a chilly, impersonal mask.

"I'm sorry, *Ms.* Littlebird, but I think you'll find my suite has been paid up through the end of the month."

"You—no, you—I didn't..." She closed her eyes and

drew a deep, deep breath. "I received no such payment."

"I left it on top of the desk in my suite. If you didn't open the envelope I specifically addressed to you, then I'm afraid the error in payment lies on your end. The room is mine."

Toni hiked her chin and glared.

Dax set his jaw in a hard, unyielding line. A layer of ice turned his eyes into bright, cold stones…much like the teal topaz pendant hanging from a gold chain around Toni's neck. She instinctively reached for the gemstone and closed her fingers around it. Having been nestled against her chest, the stone exuded more warmth than was reflected in Dax's eyes in that moment.

"Where's the envelope?" His voice sliced to her soul. Not mean, just cold, and so impersonal.

"Upstairs. Go on, Dax, get it. You win."

He turned toward the stairs, and then back. Something in his demeanor belied the rigidity of his features. "The only thing I want to 'win' is you, Littlebird. What happened…why are you so angry?"

Toni sighed. "If you have to ask, you wouldn't understand anyway." She indicated a small basket on the counter. "Leave your check here. I suppose the room is yours, if you still want it. I have things to do."

She left him standing in the foyer, shoulders slumped, looking lost and defeated. Only pure, stubborn determination got her upstairs and into her own suite of rooms before she fell apart.

Dax went straight to the desk in his room, expecting to find the envelope where he'd left it. Toni's chilly response indicated she hadn't found it, but the surface of the desk was clear of everything except a lamp, a notepad with a hummingbird logo, and an inexpensive pen.

He opened the center drawer, and his heart sank. The sketchpad lay where he'd left it, but it wasn't closed, and he always turned the cover down over the pages after a work session. His half-finished final attempt to create a chapel that had no place in Hummingbird Hollow lay face up, like a taunt to his sanity.

*This* was the answer to Toni's behavior.

Dax stared at the partially finished drawing, sickened. Who or what had taken possession of his pencil that night? What had he been thinking?

Nature dwelt in Toni's hollow in all her unblemished glory. No one used the wonderful, centuries old trees for timber, or cut jagged swaths through the forested area to create roads for their vehicles. Everything within the hollow *fit* into nature's scheme. Even this imperfect old house.

Dax cast his gaze around the room, surprised to find the irregularities in its construction no longer elicited the reaction he'd experienced upon his first arrival—that unsettled, slightly nauseated feeling in the pit of his stomach. Knowing Toni, hearing her stories about her mother and grandmother had changed the way he thought, and turned the home she shared with strangers into a warm haven. Her multiply 'great' grandfather had built the place as much like a Native American meeting house as possible—a labor of love, to help his Cherokee wife feel at home away from her people. The original dwelling, although updated and modernized by later generations, still existed at the core of the house. All the strangely placed wings and extra rooms were built around that circular core.

Having learned the home's history, Dax found himself no

longer possessed of even the slightest urge to rip it apart and start over. Toni's home had grown with past generations of the Littlebird family, and should be preserved as it was. He wouldn't want to change a thing.

Except the owner's attitude. How was he ever to explain his disappearance in a positive light? Stealing away in the night, after the magical day they'd shared…bad move. Very, very bad move.

Leaving behind those sketches of sleek, ultra-modern structures? Beyond bad, no matter how pure his intentions. Beyond stupid and thoughtless. Risking the possibility of Toni seeing the out-of-place drawings rated top billing in the list of unwise decisions ever made by D. Dax Hendrick. He knew Toni—her heart and soul—so much better than these hateful sketches represented.

*Lord, if I'm ever to win back her trust and affection, I'll need help digging my way out of this hole. Please…Daddy God?* Maybe addressing the Father the same way Toni did would soften His heart. *You know me. You see my heart and are aware of my innermost thoughts. I didn't set out to hurt Littlebird. I never, ever want to hurt her—I love her. Could You…would You help me prove myself to this beautiful, charming, unpredictable and downright cantankerous female You sent me to find?*

He sure hoped the Father was listening. Dax needed all the help he could get.

With a sigh, he looked around the room. What had happened to the envelope he'd left on the desk? On hands and knees, he searched the floor beneath the small writing table, and then under the bed—maybe when Toni opened the door, air movement picked up the envelope and dropped it somewhere.

Even as he shone his keychain flashlight into the darkness

beneath the bed skirt, he realized the futility of his actions. The envelope couldn't have blown away when the door opened. He distinctly remembered sliding one corner beneath the heavy desk lamp. Someone had removed it from the desk.

Someone like Toni. Yet she said she hadn't received the check, and Dax knew her well, despite his recent behavior. Her lips never uttered lies. She may have found the envelope, but she never opened it.

He sat on the bed and closed his eyes, imagining the possibilities.

She entered his room to check on him when he didn't come downstairs for breakfast. He'd known she'd do that, had counted on it, that's why he left the envelope for her to find. But Toni was upset. She didn't immediately open the envelope, because his unmade bed told its own story. He was gone, and she was looking for clues as to why. So she opened the desk drawer...and found the sketchpad.

Dax huffed out a breath as pain slammed his solar plexus like a physical punch. His eyes flew open as he doubled over in reaction. He'd known he and Toni were connected, but this...this connection between Toni's heart and his...it surpassed his ability to imagine.

*Oh, Littlebird. I'm so sorry, darlin'!*

He walked directly to the trash container beside the desk. Toni's pain and anger would have allowed her only one reaction in that moment—throw it all away, just as he had appeared to do.

Sure enough, there it lay, unopened, on the bottom of the trash container.

Dax picked it up, and his lips curved into a tiny, bitter grin. Never in his life had he doodled any kind of pictures around a woman's name. Not until Littlebird...and if she'd allow him the privilege of staying in her life, he'd be happy to draw whatever cutesy icons he could think of around her name every day for the rest of his life.

He dropped his duffel on the bed, retrieved his check from the envelope he'd rescued, and took it downstairs. After placing it in the basket Toni had indicated, he weighted it down with a small hummingbird figure he found on the countertop.

Then he headed for the kitchen. He'd be needing Jonathan's help.

# 11

"GOT A MINUTE, BOSS? I need to show you something."

"Of course, Jonathan. What is it?" Toni smiled at the big, kind-hearted chef who had become a dear friend.

She wasn't sure she could have handled the past few days without him. When he learned that Dax had disappeared without explanation, he took over the inn and allowed Toni the time she needed to absorb the loss.

She'd prayed and meditated, while her hummingbirds gathered around her in masses. Apparently they felt her pain, and their presence comforted her. Her dance ritual during that time became something incredibly meaningful...and subtly different, as she moved to accommodate the increased number of tiny partners.

But most of her time during those dark days was spent within the hidden cavern, wrapped in Dax's jacket. She'd found the garment on the rock bench, where he'd spread it for her the day they found the cave. Tears burst from her eyes with painful force. She'd taken a seat a good many feet away, but her gaze kept returning to the forgotten coat. At last, she was unable to resist the overwhelming desire to snuggle into it. When she did, it was as if Dax was there, with his arm around her shoulders. The garment smelled like earth and pine and something unidentifiable...something uniquely Dax.

"Toni? Are you OK?"

Jonathan's hand on her shoulder brought her back to the moment. In her mind, she'd been back in the cavern, Dax's special smell tantalizing her nostrils while hummingbirds darted and dashed and whizzed around the underground chamber in a blur of rainbow colors.

She sighed. "Yes. I'm sorry, Jon. I can't seem to keep my head in the game lately."

"I understand." His gentle voice soothed, and Toni reached out and pulled him into a quick, spontaneous hug. "Thank you for always being there for me."

He patted her shoulder. "It's what friends do, boss." He hesitated, and then gestured toward the door. "Are you ready? This shouldn't take long."

"Can you give me just a moment? I need to greet my other guests. I've been…well, you know. I really haven't given them much attention."

As she'd come through the dining room, Toni had noticed her two other guests in the dining room, looking over the selection of food in covered dishes on the warming trays. Pancakes–not her hummingbird pancakes, but nice, fluffy ones, prepared Jonathan-style. Scrambled eggs. Toast or biscuits. A nice selection of fresh fruit. Cereal and yogurt.

Her guests were a woman from California and a young Texas gentleman. When Toni entered the dining room, she found them sharing a table. Apparently they'd decided having breakfast with a stranger beat dining alone. Good. Toni encouraged interaction between her guests. That's why she kept puzzles and card games in the sunroom. Folks often left Inn the Hollow having formed new friendships that promised to be permanent. Toni had received many postcards and letters, thanking her for her hospitality and for the pleasure of meeting her other guests.

Today's visitors proved friendly and talkative. They greeted Toni with open, welcoming smiles. She offered her help if they had questions or ran into any problem in their rooms.

"I doubt there'll be a single problem, Toni." The woman, Nell, smiled and shook her head. "This place is absolutely charming. I love it here!"

"I agree," the man offered. His name was Rhett, like the "Gone with the Wind" character. He gave her the same adorably boyish grin he'd used when, while registering for his room, he'd told her his mother watched the three and a half-hour classic at least once a month. "I travel a lot, and I'm really happy to have found your place. I'll be back, for sure."

"I'm so glad you both like it here." Toni smiled. "I'll leave you to your breakfast, but don't hesitate to find me if you need anything at all."

She turned to go, and found Jonathan waiting in the doorway, drumming his fingers silently against the wall. He raised his eyebrows and jerked his head toward the kitchen.

Weird. Jonathan rarely pushed her or anyone else. One might expect a man of Jonathan's size and talent to be more assertive, but he didn't need to be. His kindness worked its magic on most folks. Those who weren't moved by that usually respected his considerable size. Either way, he rarely needed to 'push' to achieve what he wanted.

Right now, Jonathan was eager to get her out of the house and off to wherever he was taking her. She said goodbye to Nell and Rhett and joined him in the kitchen, where he immediately opened the door and ushered her outside.

She didn't ask where he was taking her. It didn't matter. Nothing mattered, really—except finding something to take Dax off her mind, which wasn't likely to happen with him here. So far today, she'd been fortunate enough not to run into him. Jonathan had told her that he breakfasted early, and then disappeared into the woods, carrying his portfolio.

Had he gone to the cavern to work? Toni couldn't help

wondering, but she blocked the picture of his head bent over a sketchpad—or whatever he used when actually working—with one little unruly lock of hair continually falling over his forehead. The geyser in front of him. The hummingbirds flitting around the geyser, and perhaps paying an occasional visit to the quiet man on the sidelines.

Enough. This wasn't working.

"Where are we going, Jonathan?"

"We're almost there, boss."

She started to insist on a full explanation, and then sighed. Why bother? Let him take her wherever he had in mind, show her whatever he thought she needed to see. On the way back, she would ask Jonathan to take over the B & B for a month. She had no idea where she'd go, but she had to get away from here. Now that she'd shown Dax over every possible inch of the hollow, not a single place remained in which she wouldn't encounter his memory upon every return visit.

Jonathan stopped. Toni didn't. She walked right into his broad back and bounced backward.

"Toni!" Jonathan swung around, wide-eyed, but he couldn't have prevented her from falling.

Someone else did.

Instead of meeting the ground rear first, Toni fell against a broad, unyielding chest. A pair of strong arms circled her from behind.

"Whoa there, darlin'!"

"Dax!"

Pleasant tingles started in her midsection and radiated up and down her entire body. As much as she longed to relax into his embrace, she jerked free.

"Th—thank you." She set about smoothing her top and skirt, neither of which required any attention.

"Any time, Littlebird."

"Well, uhm..I gotta get back to the house. See ya later, boss."

Before Toni could catch her breath, Jonathan was off and gone, long strides returning him to the kitchen.

Traitor!

She lifted her gaze and found a twinkling teal one waiting.

"I suppose you had him bring me here?"

"Of course I did."

"Why? I need my chef, Dax. I'd hate to have to fire him on your account."

"You won't fire Jonathan, Littlebird. I know you better than that."

"You don't know me at all!" she spat.

"I know you think I don't, and believe me, I'm about as sorry as a man can get. But I refuse to just go away, because I love you too much. Besides, I worked really hard to get this ready for you. At the very least, you have to hear me out before you send me packing."

She hesitated. "And after I 'hear you out,' you'll go away and leave me alone?"

"If you still want me to."

"Oh, I will."

He held out a hand. "Fine. We'll see. For now, please…come with me."

She stared at his hand, even raised hers in response. Then she dropped it back to her side. "Let's get it over with then. I'll follow you."

He sighed and shook his head. "You are the stubbornest woman I've ever known."

"Which has nothing to do with this, does it? Just take me where we're going…or are we through here?"

"Look, darlin', you're going to have to take my hand, because…" He pulled a long scarf out of his hip pocket. "I'm blindfolding you."

She gasped. "You most certainly are not!"

He grinned. "You can let me do it, or I'll hold you down and do it anyway." The obnoxious grin broadened. "Actually, I kinda wish you'd give me a fight. That might be fun."

She shot him a withering glare. "I'm not going to wrestle with you, Dax. Just get it over with, so we can go back to the house. I'm looking forward to watching you and your stupid horses ride away."

He chuckled. "You are feisty. Who'da thunk?" Then, in a flash, he had the scarf over her eyes and around her head. "Tell me if it's too tight."

"It's fine, you big bully." Even after he'd hurt and disappointed her, Toni wasn't afraid to be alone with him—in the woods, and blindfolded. "Can we go now?"

"Sure. May I lead you, or are you going to make me pick you up and carry you?"

"I'll let you lead me. But whatever it is you're showing me had better be good enough to make me forget what a brute you are."

"All right. Here we go." He took her hand and guided it to his shoulder. "I'm going to turn around. Just keep a hold on my shoulder. It'll only be for a moment."

Toni's grip on his shoulder tightened as soon as he took a step.

"It's okay, darlin'. Just take it slow and easy."

His deep voice calmed and guided her, and he'd been truthful—within a moment, he stopped.

"We're here. Now, just stand..." He positioned her right where he wanted her, then took a gentle hold on her chin. "Just relax. I'm going to turn your face so you're looking right at it."

"Right at what?"

"Patience, Littlebird!" He chuckled. "I need to have a chat with your hummers and let them know what they should teach you next." He stepped back, and Toni wanted to kick herself when a wave of loss swept over her. "Okay, here goes." His fingers touched the back of her head and fiddled with the scarf a bit.

The cloth fell away.

# 12

"OHHHH!"

What else does one say upon the realization of a long-held dream?

Toni didn't know she was crying until Dax brushed the tears off her cheek with one finger.

"I'll start over, darlin'. Please don't cry."

Toni gasped. "You'll do *what*? Don't you dare change a thing! This is—it's beyond perfect!"

"But you're—" He touched her cheek again. "You're crying."

A soft, breathy laugh was all she could manage, so she shook her head and cupped his face in her hands. "I'm crying because you know me so well. This chapel is exactly what I've dreamed of, only I didn't have the vision to actually see it. Now that I have, I know it's what belongs here—right here in this spot. It's perfect, Dax."

He pulled her close, and she wrapped both arms around his waist. A slight tremble in his body broke her heart. Without asking, she knew he'd been afraid she'd reject his touch.

"So are you, darlin'." His deep voice rumbled in his chest and tingled against her ear. "I've never seen anything more perfect than you."

"How can you say that after the way I treated you?" She kept hold of his waist, but raised her head to meet his gaze. "I'm not perfect. Not by a long shot."

"You can take that up with Daddy God if you think you need to, but for now, my heart tells me you're perfect."

"Mine tells me that you've outdone yourself with this…perfect presentation."

He twisted his lips to the side and scrunched one eye shut. "You like it, then?"

"I love it, D. Dax."

They were in the small glade they'd once crossed together to get to the cave—except now, the clearing was a little less than clear.

A chapel stood against the hillside.

"How did you…?" She shook her head. The structure had not been there the day before.

"Well, it's portable—mostly high-grade cardboard and plexiglass. It'll come down in a few minutes, but I wanted you to actually see a 3D version of what I came up with for your dream chapel."

"I love it. But…" She hesitated, shaking her head. "I don't understand. I saw your sketches, and they weren't…*this*."

"Oh, Littlebird. I'm sorry you saw those. I think some demon of division got hold of my pencil that night." His lips stretched into something more grimace than grin. "At some point I came to myself and realized how far off I was. Not one of those drawings depicted anything that belonged in Hummingbird Hollow, and they certainly weren't a good fit for my little hummingbird whisperer."

She nodded. "When I saw them, I was shattered, because what they said to me was—" Toni broke off, drew a deep breath, and lifted her gaze to his. "That you didn't know me at all. Not even a little."

A muscle in Dax's jaw clenched and unclenched. "I'm so sorry, darlin'. Those drawings are not entirely mine. I don't know how to explain it, but I know—and you know, if you'll allow yourself to remember *us*—that I would never have presented those sketches as even remote possibilities for your chapel." He took her hand. "Come take a closer look."

They approached the small, round structure. Round, like the home her ancestor had built for the wife he adored. Glass, like Thorncrown Chapel, so the building introduced as little intrusion on nature as possible. The roof....

Looking at the top of the chapel, Toni's eyes misted yet again. Dax had taken time to research historical Cherokee homes. The little glass chapel wore a crown of what appeared to be bark, covered with long blades of grass.

Dax slipped an arm around her waist. "Modern roofing materials will be hidden beneath the bark and grass. Your little house of worship will stand secure against wind and rain. But I wanted to incorporate the earthy materials your ancestors once used, as well. Of course, if you don't like the look..."

"I know I'm repeating myself, but words fail me, Dax. It's perfect. The roof. The shape. The materials. Please don't change anything about it."

"Not a chance. This is yours, darlin'. It'll be built your way."

"Can we go inside?"

He grinned. "I thought you'd never ask."

He led her to the door. Toni chuckled when she saw what was tucked into the cardboard handle.

"The envelope you left for me."

"Yes. There's something inside."

"But you put the check in the lobby basket."

"Yes, I did."

"Oh..." She drew a deep breath. "You left an explanation, didn't you? If I'd only opened the envelope..."

"You still can."

She nodded and slipped a single sheet of paper from its

hiding place.

*Littlebird ~*

*I listened to your song tonight...drank in your beautiful face as you sang...and my heart spoke to me. It said, "Design her dream." You haven't told me much about that dream, but in the few words you did say, I heard an entire lifetime of longing. I can't give you that dream without going home for a few days, and the sooner I'm gone, the faster I can get back.*
*I love you, darlin'. Please don't imagine any awful reason that I'm leaving without a goodbye, because there isn't one, other than to make you happy when I return.*

*With all my heart,*
*With all my love,*
*D. Dax Hendrick*

"I'm so, so sorry." She raised a hand to cover her trembling lips, and then dropped it to look at him—face to face, eye to eye. "I'm the one who failed to know the man I love. I'll work on that, if you'll let me."

"Let you? Littlebird, that would make me the happiest man in the world." He carefully swung the makeshift door open. "I know I'm late but...Happy Valentine's Day, darlin'. Welcome to Hummingbird Chapel."

Inside the circular structure, quiet ruled. No whispering breeze. No chirping birds or chattering squirrels. No low roar of planes flying overhead.

Dax hadn't included interior plans in his portable showpiece, but Toni's creative mind started working on that without a second's hesitation.

"It's going to be a haven, Dax. Simple—I don't want a lot

of furniture or decorative items. The chapel should be dedicated to prayer and meditation." That made her think about her usual prayer time, and she paused, nibbling at her lip. "What about my hummingbirds, Dax?"

He grinned. "I thought about them as well. Look at this."

At the rear of the structure—backed up against a hill that sheltered a secret, underground spring—a small, square 'room' jutted out from the rounded wall by less than a foot. Glass, like the chapel, it would be all but unnoticeable to a casual observer.

Dax approached the small addition and opened two sliding windows, one on each side. "If you work a good many flowering plants into your interior design, your little friends will come inside through these openings."

Toni couldn't stop smiling. "I will give them ample flowers to feed on, of course. But they'd come anyway. They love our prayer time."

He shook his head. "Do you have any idea what a special, amazing, beautiful...*perfect* woman I've fallen in love with?"

She slid her arms around his neck. "I can't say I've thought about that, but would you like me to tell you about the wonderful, handsome, kind and talented man I love?"

Dax drew her close and bent his head close to hers. His warm breath brushed her lips, hiking her body temperature into what had to be some kind of danger zone. "I'd love to hear what you have to say about that guy, but..." His lips across hers—a teasing, barely there, almost kiss. "Not right now. Sometimes talking is overrated."

She laughed. "I couldn't agree more. So kiss me already."

He gathered her into his arms. The fingers of one hand spread across the back of Toni's head and drew her face as close as possible to his.

He kissed her then—a no-holds-barred journey over her

lips that said, "I'm in this for good. All the way. Forever and ever amen."

Toni lost herself in his nearness, in the racing beat of his heart against hers, in his warmth…the smell of him…the gentleness in his touch.

They drew apart when something flew past their heads with a loud buzz.

"How did they—?" Toni stopped and shook her head.

Tiny birds filled the chapel, flying in circles around the inside perimeter of the see-through walls.

"Tchik, tchik, tchik."

"Tchuk, tchuk."

"Tsip, tsip. Zhi zhi zhi."

A medley of chirps and chips…various languages from different species filled the air.

Toni and Dax provided the only place for the birds to rest. The two soon found themselves covered in tiny, brightly hued birds.

"This…isn't…happening. Is it?" Dax's low, reverent whisper drew Toni's gaze to his.

She smiled. "My friends are expressing their approval of…*us*. I hope you don't mind."

"Mind?" He closed his eyes. "I've never experienced anything quite so overpowering, darlin'. Hummingbirds all over my body, and you in my arms. Heaven can't possibly be any better."

"I'd like you to kiss me again, D. Dax, while the hummingbirds are singing our song. But first…about that D…"

Dax chuckled. "I won't make you promise not to laugh, because you will. In my parent's defense, it was my maternal grandmother's maiden name, and my folks are more family-oriented than most." He rolled his eyes, shook his head. A wave of color rolled up his neck and into his face. Despite the beard, his face glowed brick red.

"It can't be that bad." Toni almost regretted pushing him to share.

"Worse. Darling."

Toni laughed. "What did I do to deserve that ending 'g'? I kind of liked 'darlin'.'"

Dax shook his head and raised his gaze to the top of the room. "I wasn't calling you darling, darlin'."

"But you said—" Her eyes went so wide it almost hurt. "The D...?"

He nodded. "Yep. You got it."

Toni smiled. She traced his mouth with her finger, and raised her face, offering him her lips again.

"I love it, and I love you, my Darling Dax. Now, kiss me again, please."

"You are aware that we're both still wearing hummingbirds, right?"

"Mmm-hmmm." She tiptoed, touched her lips to the corner of his. "We'll call this one our first hummingbird kiss. Don't you want to know how it feels?"

He growled a little, and Toni gasped. Her heart jumped. Her tummy turned upside down. Body and soul strained toward his.

"Here's to Hummingbird Chapel." Dax dipped his head to kiss the tip of her nose, and then hovered a mere breath away from her lips. "And this..." He danced his lips across hers again. "...is to a lifetime of hummingbird kisses."

He claimed his kiss then. No more teasing, barely there lip dances. This one weakened Toni's knees and turned her tummy upside down.

She smiled and Dax drew away, just enough to tantalize.

"What?"

"I like hummingbird kisses, my Darling Dax. Maybe next we can try a Harley hug?"

"Whatever you say, Littlebird. Just don't say it now."

Toni shushed when the next kiss stole her voice and every lucid thought.

The hummingbirds rose, as one, and darted outside through their specially designed windows.

Toni paid them no mind. They'd come again, with more sweet kisses. Today, they'd brought a special blessing on a lifetime of tomorrows.

# Hummingbird Pancakes

**Ingredients:**

    1½ cups baking mix (e.g., Bisquick)
    ½ tsp ground cinnamon
    1½ cup half and half
    1 large, very ripe banana, mashed
    1/3 cup drained, crushed pineapple
    1/4 cup sugar
    3 T butter, melted
    1 large egg
    ¼ cup finely chopped pecans (optional)

**Directions:**

Heat griddle or skillet over medium heat.

In large bowl, combine baking mix and cinnamon.

In another bowl, whisk together everything else (except pecans).

Stir wet and dry ingredients together, just until moistened. Do not over mix.

Fold in pecans (optional)

Poor batter, ¼ cup for each pancake, onto pre-heated griddle (or skillet), moistened with butter or coconut oil. Cook 2-4 minutes. When top side bubbles and edges start to look dry, turn and cook 2-3 minutes more, until done. Serve with warm cream cheese anglaise (recipe follows) or coconut syrup.

**Suggested garnishes:**

Thinly sliced bananas

Chunks of pineapple

Scatterings of toasted coconut

Fresh fruit

### Cream Cheese Anglaise

- 1 ½ cups half and half
- ½ (8-oz.) pkg cream cheese (4 oz.), softened
- 1/3 to 1/2 cup sugar (This depends on how sweet you prefer your pancake topping. My hubby prefers the larger amount.)
- 3 egg yolks
- 1 T cornstarch
- 1/8 tsp salt
- 2 T butter
- 1 tsp vanilla

**Instructions:**

Place everything except butter and vanilla in a blender. Process until smooth, and transfer to a medium saucepan. Bring mixture to a boil over medium heat, whisking constantly. Continue to whisk constantly while boiling for 1 minute. Remove from heat and whisk in butter and vanilla. Serve immediately.

# Bells on Her Toes

(Love at Christmas Inn,
Collection I)

*"Make pomegranates of blue, purple and scarlet yarn
around the hem of the robe, with gold bells between them.
The gold bells and the pomegranates are to alternate around
the hem of the robe. Aaron must wear it when he ministers.
The sound of the bells will be heard when he enters the Holy
Place before the Lord…" ~Exodus 28:33-35 (NIV)~*

# 1

**"WE'RE EARLY." KARYNN MICHAELS GLANCED** at her cell phone screen. "By a whole two hours. How could we have over-estimated driving time by that much?"

"We didn't." Her sister swung her luxury sedan into a small shopping center a few blocks from their destination and slid smoothly into a parking slot. She shot Karynn an impish grin and opened her door. "I got us here early so you could get a head start on unwrapping your gift."

"Savannah!" She climbed out, and then stood for a second, listening for the beep that assured her the doors were locked.

"What are you up to now?"

Her gaze swept the storefronts lined up side by side. The little strip mall boasted only a half dozen or so businesses. Which of them was her sister all set to dash into and lay down more money?

Savannah could afford to spend lavishly, now that she'd married Dr. Darren Quinn, brain surgeon extraordinaire. Karynn rejoiced in the couple's happiness and was thrilled for her sister—who grew up right along with her in the school of hard knocks, hard work and staying hard at it to keep the wolves from the door.

Still, despite her genuine joy in Savannah's happiness and financial security, she cringed when the younger woman tossed money around like game board cash. This trip to Hope Creek, for instance. Why couldn't her sister be like everyone else and just wrap up a bathrobe or a good book for her birthday? But no…nothing would do but to bring Karynn here—several hours from their hometown of Quillpoint—for a ten-day vacation at Christmas Inn. They'd be in Hope Creek all the way through Karynn's birthday on December 25th. Darren would join them on Christmas Eve.

She didn't dare think about the fact that Hearth & Home, the bed and breakfast that was her livelihood, would be closed for two entire weeks. She'd manage the loss of income by cutting corners for a while. Growing up poor taught a person how to live on less than most people thought possible.

Savannah rounded the hood of the car and pulled her into a tight hug. "Sis, just let me do this for you. Please? Darren *wants* me to. He gave me specific instructions to pull out all the stops and show you the time of your life." She batted her long lashes like a preening prima donna. "He said he owes you for taking such awesome care of his 'Precious' until he could take over."

They both burst out laughing, despite the truth of the exaggerated presentation. Dr. Quinn adored his wife and always referred to her as 'my Precious,' never mind the negative connotations brought about in recent years by a popular book-turned-movie. Unlike Karynn, Darren didn't waste time and effort trying to please everyone.

Savannah grabbed her hand and tugged her along as she stepped out of the parking slot and onto a wide sidewalk. "Seriously, Karynn, my husband thinks you're pretty special, and he's right. You are. So this year, we want to pamper you for your birthday. Will you just let us do that without fretting the entire time?"

"Oh, sweetie…I promise to try, but you know how I am." Karynn heaved a hopeless sigh. "If life were to roll along without a single kink in the works, I'd fret because there's nothing to fret about."

"Well, then I'll consider it my job to foil your frets. See this?" Savannah whirled in a circle and pivoted to a stop directly in front of Karynn, who came close to barreling into her.

"Vanna!" She brushed off her sweater, which didn't need brushing. Still, it made her feel better to administer a stinging slap to *something*.

"Sorry, Sis. But look at me." Savannah tilted her head forward, raised one perfect eyebrow and dipped the other one. "When you see me do this, you'll know you're being an old fuddy-duddy fretter."

"What are you, eight years old?" Karynn tried to give her sister a stern look, but when Savannah only repeated the 'fuddy-duddy' alert, she burst out laughing instead. "Fine. I will try to behave more like my crazy, lighthearted, totally irresponsible little sister. Now, will you stop doing that?" She cast a furtive glance around. "People will think you're strange."

"Uh-uh…that's fretting!" Still, Savannah stopped rolling her eyes, linked arms with Karynn and they were on the move again. "Anyway, I am strange."

"Well, you got that right." Karynn giggled, and then blinked. Twice. *Giggling? Really? Now who's the eight-year-old?*

"This is it!" Savannah trilled. "We're here."

Karynn read the sign on the window and suppressed a sigh.

*Nail It.*

"I take it we're getting manicures?"

"And pedicures—a double-digits treat. And we're right on time for our appointment." She opened the door, enacted an exaggerated bow, and waved Karynn inside with a flourish. "After you, birthday girl!"

****

Later that evening, Karynn started to slip one foot into a brand new, strappy red heel, but paused to consider. She loved the shoes, in spite of the scary price tag they'd worn when she spotted them. But the bright, cheery bells, one on each of her toes….

"Maybe I should wear something else. Don't get me wrong…I loved the mani-pedi, but my sweet, little Bohemian toe tickler might have gone a bit over the top. I'm not sure I want to hang these showy toes out there for everyone to see."

"*What?* No way, Sis. You're wearing those heels. And your toes look fabulous!" She crossed the room to stand in front of Karynn. The silver sequins around her dipping neckline caught the light and sent out a myriad of bright sparkles as she moved. "Honey, they're not gaudy at all. You asked for a soft, nearly transparent background. What's so showy about that? And the bells are beautiful—not large or distasteful in any way. You look stunning, Karynn, and I love that your finger-and-toe designs match so perfectly."

Karynn sighed and slipped on the shoes. Savannah would throw a fit if she refused to wear them, and it wasn't worth an argument. At least her hands sported tiny bells only on the ring fingers.

Moving to the full-length mirror, she took in her completed look for the formal dinner downstairs. She hadn't dressed up for anything in such a long time…maybe this was too much.

"Oh, no, you don't." Her sister stepped up beside her and used the fuddy-duddy alert for the first time since they'd left the salon. "You look absolutely beautiful. Not in the least pretentious or overdressed." She laughed when Karynn's eyes widened. "What? I've known you all my life, remember? You always think you have to live in someone else's shadow. Well, not tonight. Tonight you shine!"

Savannah reached up to touch Karynn's hair, arranged in a loose coil behind one ear, with wispy strands hanging free. Tiny, pearl-tipped pins sparkled from within the twist.

"You look like Italian royalty. Do you seriously not know how lovely you are?" She kissed Karynn's cheek—lightly. "Don't want to mess up the little touch of makeup you allowed yourself. Thing is, on you it's enough. You look amazing completely *au naturale*, but this—a bare touch of cosmetics to highlight your beauty—it's perfect." She shook her head. "I can't believe some guy hasn't scooped you up and carried you away, long ago."

"Oh, stop it." Karynn gave her sister a quick hug, and then ran both hands over the deep red fabric that hugged her hips and flowed like a silky river to her ankles. "I don't need a man to sweep me off my feet, and I'd never leave Quillpoint.

You're the only family I've got, kiddo. You're stuck with me."

"Hmmm…what if Daniel showed up again?"

A quick intake of air, and then Karynn regained the composure she'd lost for half a second. "If Daniel had wanted to return, he would have by now. Let's not talk about him."

"Then let's talk about the box of Daniel-memories you still keep in your closet."

She rolled her eyes and busied herself putting on a pair of her sister's triple-strand diamond earrings. Savannah had insisted they—and the matching necklace—were perfect accessories for her outfit, but Karynn wouldn't be comfortable until the expensive trinkets were back in the safe.

"Savannah…"

"I know, I know. But tell me about them, and I'll leave it alone." Savannah settled on the side of her bed to watch Karynn finish getting ready. "Although…" She lowered her voice to a mutter. "I think I know why every single man who's tried to win you over in the past decade has 'lacked that certain something.'"

Karynn chuckled. She'd almost heard herself in Savannah's silly impression. "Oh, do you now?"

"Yep. That 'certain something' they all lacked? They weren't Daniel Sheridan."

Karynn turned to face her pesky sister, both earrings swinging. "What does it matter?"

"It matters because you have to move on, Sis. Or maybe we could find Daniel!" Savannah's blue eyes took on a gleam that knotted every nerve in Karynn's body. "We'll hire a private investigator and—"

"Savannah! Listen to yourself!" Karynn snatched up the soft, white wrap spread across her bed and pulled it over her shoulders. "Daniel was my high school sweetheart. He and his family left, and we eventually lost contact. It happens. We were kids, honey."

She perched on the edge of the bed and took her sister's hand. "I keep the box in my closet because it holds memories that are still sweet, even though things didn't work out for Daniel and me—not because I'm still weeping over him, or dreaming of the day he returns." She stood, tugging the younger woman up beside her. "Now let's go down to dinner."

"OK." Savannah crossed to the mirror for one last look at herself. "Oh, wait! You're supposed to ring your bell."

Karynn's 'Bells on Her Toes' mani-pedi package had included a beautiful handheld crystal bell…and a series of ten 'promidictions'—some promises, some cheesy predictions. She'd been instructed by the petite, flower-child pedicurist to ring the crystal bell once a day, after reading that day's 'wise words.' Karynn preferred to call it a daily slice of absurdity.

"You don't expect me to play along with that silly bell-ringing ritual?"

"It'll be fun!" Savannah reached for the box in which the crystal bell resided. "May I?"

"Knock yourself out."

Savannah lifted the bell from its satin bed. "It's lovely."

"Yes." *And a good part of why that mani-pedi package was so expensive.* Karynn bit down on her bottom lip, and then made a deliberate decision to share something of herself with her sister. "You know, there's a bell in that box of 'Daniel-memories' in my closet. Just a cheap, glass one, but Daniel gave it to me the day he left Quillpoint." She stared off into the corner of the room, remembering how he'd used his thumb to brush away her tears, and pulled her in for a sweet kiss before he handed her the bell. "He said to ring it and think of him when I was lonely."

"Did you?"

"Many times." Karynn tucked a small, sequined clutch under her arm and headed for the door. "But he mustn't have heard, because ringing that bell never brought him back. After a while, he didn't even call anymore. Let's go eat."

"First you have to ring this. I insist—and read the first promidiction."

Karynn laughed and joined Savannah in the vanity area.

Ten small envelopes lay beneath the satin cushion on which the bell had rested. Karynn removed a single half-sheet of paper from the one marked "Today," and read the beautiful, flowing script aloud, for Savannah's benefit. *"You will come into contact with someone from your past. Whether the relationship was romantic, familial, or a simple friendship, its revival will impact your future in unforgettable ways."*

Karynn rolled her eyes, but she picked up the bell and swung it back and forth, enjoying the sweet, high tinkle in spite of the ridiculous situation. "There. Now let's go." She reclaimed her evening bag and widened her eyes. "Perhaps this mystery person waits in the dining room even now."

Savannah gave her another fuddy-duddy face, but said no more.

The sisters admired the lovely Christmas decorations as they made their way downstairs. A dainty garland of holly berries and silver bells wound around the baluster, from the newel post at the top to the identical one at the bottom of the staircase. Over the fireplace, a large clock boasted elves that popped out every quarter hour to chase each other behind the timepiece and back inside.

Darren's family had wonderful memories of Christmas Inn, where they'd often spent brief vacations. "It never mattered what time of year we were there," he had told them. "The place is like having Christmas all year round. It's beautiful, and the décor is breathtaking. I was a kid—and a boy, so I didn't really notice particulars, but it did make an impression. You girls will love it."

Karynn did love it. While retaining the all-important elements of welcome and home, the inn also possessed an unmistakable touch of class. She was eager to explore the gift shop. Perhaps she'd find something to enhance those same elements at Hearth & Home.

A faint smell of paint, varnish and new carpet hung in the air, lending a clean, fresh ambiance. Had the place fallen into disrepair at some point? Many clues pointed to a recent facelift...but then, Karynn's efforts to maintain her bed and breakfast made her aware that keeping a place like Christmas Inn in this kind of condition would be a constant, ongoing effort.

"This is it." Savannah spoke in an awed tone, so unlike her usual fun-at-all-costs persona that Karynn bit back a grin. Her sister was impressed with their surroundings, as well.

They stood in the door of the dining room, getting their bearings.

White linen cloths topped six round tables, each of which boasted a three-arm candelabrum. Candlelight played over bright Christmas baubles and gleaming silverware.

"Each table has its own holiday theme," Savannah noted.

Karynn lifted an eyebrow. "And each room is assigned to a specific table, based on theme?"

"Right. Ours is the bell theme." She laughed. "So is our room—and your toes. We'll be hearing bells in our sleep tonight, won't we?"

Karynn glanced down at the painted-on bells peeking from beneath the hem of her gown. They were growing on her. "That's OK. I like them. Let's find our table." She gave Savannah a quick, mischievous grin. "Or perhaps we should close our eyes and follow the sound of tinkling bells."

"Ha! I'm game, but you'd never make such a spectacle of yourself. Oh, I see it." Savannah pointed out a table that sported a bell-adorned wreath around the base of its candelabrum. "Only one other guest at our table, at least for now."

An older gentleman stood as they approached, a broad smile lighting his face. "Ladies." He pulled a chair out for each of them before returning to his own. "I am Gabriel D'Angelo."

They introduced themselves and Gabriel shone that sunny smile again. "It is an honor to meet such lovely sisters."

Karynn couldn't put a finger on why, but the man's presence calmed her. Gabriel D'Angelo wasn't just any sweet, elderly man from...where? Certainly not America, judging by his beautiful accent. She'd enjoy getting to know this guest.

"Gabriel, I'm guessing you are perhaps from...Italy?"

"Ahh...you are as perceptive as you are lovely. Venice."

"I thought so. What brings you to Tennessee?"

"I've come to deliver a message for an old friend." He smiled, but seemed disinclined to reveal more about his mission.

Karynn didn't pry. The man's purpose in Hope Creek was his own business.

"Savannah, may I be so presumptuous as to guess that you are a newlywed?" Gabriel ventured.

Savannah laughed outright. "How did you know?"

"It is easy to see beneath the surface, if one tries. You are quite young, yet you wear a beautiful wedding ring. You are glowing, so your heart is happy. It was a reasonably safe assumption."

"You had me going for a second!" Savannah said. "I was starting to think—"

A petulant female voice cut into their conversation. "I take it this is the bell table."

Something unpleasant coiled its way up Karynn's spine, and her breath caught in her throat. She'd experienced it before…the same instinctive, soul-deep, gut-wrenching aversion on first contact with an individual. Over time, she'd come to recognize the powerful inner reaction as more than the instant dislike some humans experience now and then toward one another. This wasn't a personality clash or adverse chemistry. Karynn called them Spirit-warnings, and she no longer downplayed their existence or their importance. They'd proven true and accurate one hundred percent of the time.

She fisted both hands, as if by tensing her fingers she could school her facial muscles to hide the war raging inside. Then she lifted her eyes to see what kind of person could call forth her Spirit-warrior by voice alone.

Copper-colored hair. Green eyes—up-tilted, almond shaped and narrowed to slits, like a cat on the hunt. A face that might have been lovely but for its bored, dissatisfied, self-indulgent expression. The newcomer held the hand of a small, blonde-haired girl whose sunny smile made up for her mother's lack of one.

"Please…join us." Gabriel stood once again and waved an arm toward the empty chairs.

"Thank you, but we're waiting for my daddy." The child's voice was as sweet as her smile.

"I'm here, Chrissy." A tall man with a trim, medium brown beard and slightly longish hair strode toward the table. "It's crazy cold out there, and the snow is—" He broke off and stopped as if frozen in place, sapphire-blue eyes wide, shocked…and fixed on Karynn.

"I, uh…I don't…Karynn? Karynn Michaels?"

The cat-eyed woman cast a waspish look at Karynn, and

then back at her husband.

Savannah's soft laughter held a touch of pure wonder. "This is unreal."

Karynn refused to look at her sister. She forced a smile that felt wooden and dredged up every ounce of courage she possessed to hold the man's startled gaze. She prayed her eyes did not reflect the mixed emotions creating utter turmoil in her heart.

"Hello, Daniel. It's been a long time."

## Author's Note

Thank you for reading *Hummingbird Kisses*. If you enjoyed this novella, please consider leaving a short review on Amazon, Goodreads, Barnes & Noble, and/or any other site where books are read, discussed or sold. Positive reviews and word-of-mouth recommendations honor an author while also helping fellow readers find quality fiction to read.

Thank you so much!

If you'd like to receive information on new releases, please follow me here:

**www.amazon.com/author/delialatham**.

# About the Author

Writing Heaven's touch into earthly tales, **Delia Latham** puts her characters through the fire of earthly trials to bring them out victorious by the hand of God, His heavenly messengers, and good, old-fashioned love. You'll always find a touch of the divine in her tales of sweet romance.

Delia lives in East Texas with her husband Johnny. She's a Christian wife, mother, grandmother, sister, friend, and author of inspirational romance…with a finger or two immersed in the design pool, where she creates beautiful marketing material for other authors. She treasures her role as child of the King and heir to the throne of God. She's got a "thing" for Dr. Pepper and *loves* hearing from readers.

Contact this author at any of the following locations:
**www.delialatham.net**
**www.amazon.com/author/delialatham**
**www.facebook.com/delialatham**

Subscribe to Delia's newsletter, Brushing Wings:
**https://www.subscribepage.com/BrushingWings**

# More Titles by Delia Latham

## Paradise Pines

*Never the Twain* (Book 1)
*Like a Dance* (Book 2)

## Paradise Pines

*Winter Wonders* (#4)
*Autumn Falls* (#3)
*Summer Dreams* (#2)
*Spring Raine* (#1)

## Heart's Haven Novellas

*Jewels for the Kingdom*
*Lexi's Heart*
*Love in the WINGS*

*A Cowboy Christmas*
*Oh, Baby!*

## Pure Amore

*A Christmas Beau*
*At First Sight*
*Jingle Belle*

*Love at Christmas Inn: Collection I*

## A Smoky Mountain Christmas

*Do You See What I See?*

## Solomon's Gate

*Destiny's Dream* (Book One)
*Kylie's Kiss* (Book Two)
*Gypsy's Game* (Book Three)

*Lea's Gift* (Bonus Christmas story)

## Stand-alone Titles

*The First Noelle*
*Treehouse* (Short Story)
*Yesterday's Promise*
*Goldeneyes*

## Children's Picture Book

*Mine!*